Pumpkins and
PAINT

A collection of stories

☛ John Glass ☚

Student Plays
24415 Marquis Court
Laguna Hills, CA 92653
www.studentplays.org

Edited by Custer Services, Inc.
Student Plays, john@studentplays.org.
ISBN 978-0-9988523-7-9

This book is dedicated to my mother, Lana Kershner, and to the unending grace and love of my Lord Jesus Christ.

<u>CONTENTS</u>

1

Holly and the Hindenburg

Off we go, a couple of bad-ass broads with bits of a blimp in the back. We crammed the cross-braces into the trunk of my Cutlass, threw a heavy tarp over the top, and slammed the lid with a thunk. Hit 495 with a tankful of gas, money on our minds, and the purpose of a pope.

Any doofus could seize a random piece of metal from a junkyard and claim some historical significance. But this was the real deal and the detailed markings etched on the inside hull of our four stolen beauties said so: *LZ 129 Hindenburg: Deutsche - Reed-eri.* There was even a hand-sized German flag imprinted on each piece, right alongside the writing.

"Girl, this is gonna bring us two-thousand dollars!" Jackie said as we hauled the blackened steel out of the back room of the antique warehouse towards my car. Jackie: a thirty-something paint contractor, a big-boned girl with thick, luscious hair that never seems to have a speck of paint in it. Jackie, nothing more than a bar associate, someone with whom I exchange rants over life and men the few times a month I'm able to sneak off for a few drinks. Someone that showed up at the right time in my miserable existence.

But she's also someone that is now making me really question this partnership. Or whatever it is.

"This thing go any faster, Hol?" Jackie asks, giving me that sideways look.

She's sucking on a huge joint and blowing pot all over the damn place. Though the last thing we need is to get pulled over, I press another five miles an hour into the speedometer, in no mood to hear more whining.

"Yeah," I mutter. "Sure."

Whining, I've learned in the last few hours, is something that she excels at. That, along with the loud laughter and the wailing sarcasm. I'm learning more and more about this woman, and I can't say it's a settling feeling. I look through the window to my left, a smattering of telephone poles and pines, like a row of tall wooden dominoes, shooshing right by us.

Back to this thing called my existence. Yeah, it sucks, and there's no other way to put it. I'm tired of tending the books and answering the phone at my nineteen-thousand-a-year job. *Nelson Building Supply, this is Holly, can I help you?* Sick of living in Jersey, of not being able to provide. Nick, my five-year-old, needs to go to the dentist. We're out of groceries. The bank keeps calling because of the money I borrowed to pay for my last two semesters at Jersey State College. And the CHECK ENGINE light in my car comes to life whenever it wants. I look at the dim panel now, airmail a prayer that it remains that way, and then think about the bills that I'll pay once we get the loot.

Twelve hours until time to pick up Nick from a sleepover. Twelve hours to unload this scrap crap, collect our dough, and high-tail it back to Hoboken. Is this how common thieves thought? *Unload, collect, spend, repeat.* When Jackie first told me of her discovery I could barely remember the Hindenburg. It was one night at the bar, and she gushed over her Coors Light, the potential worth of her find giving fire to her eyes.

"You know, it's that famous blimp that caught on fire and crashed in Lakehurst, way back when. At least, that's what my roomie's encyclopedia says."

It took a minute but images of the fiery disaster eventually came to me. "How the hell did you come across it?"

It was on her second night on the job, Jackie said, and she had just finished up spraying primer over the entire back room when a small closet off in the corner got her attention.

"I'm working over-night so nobody but me is in there. And I'm a nosy-Rosie by nature so I just walked over, jiggled the doorknob, and *boom*, it was wide open. There were a couple of big-ass crates in there, full of antique junk. And there the blimp pieces were, lying on the very top. I think they were probably about to be moved out to the main floor."

She set her empty bottle down on the damp bar tile with a light bang, shoved the brown bangs back out of her eyes. "Anyway, I did a little research the next morning, then made a few phone calls. And now, dear Holly," she said, narrowing her mischievous eyes at me with that *you know* look. "I just need the right person to assist me."

The worn-out underbelly of my Cutlass creaks and sways as we storm on through the Jersey night at a steady seventy-eight. Now we're really in the sticks. Lake Hopatcong. Hordtown. Woodport. I'm envisioning Nick in the backseat, sitting there, observing this pair of harebrained loons. But Jackie's talking again, loudly. She's the loudest girl I've ever known.

"Another eighty miles of podunkness and we're there." She's bent over a large road map, aided by the flickering light of the visor flap, something that—like everything else in the car—is probably on its last leg.

I ask her to tell me where we're going again.

"The great town of Hainesville, New Jersey," she says, shooting another wisp of weed in my general direction. She picks up a wrinkled index card from the center console, squints at it. "A little place called Arthur's Attic."

"And what's this guy's name?"

"Frank. Said he'd wait for us until one a.m. He told me it should be a cinch since it's right off the 15. His shop is basically right under a big Pepsi billboard."

She pauses and holds the joint out as if in inspection, then exhales yet another blast of dope, which settles across the windshield and dashboard. "Don't worry. Like I told you, we'll be back long before sunrise. Back in plenty of time for you to pick up the little bastard." She throws an elbow into my side and giggles; I bite the inside of my cheek until I taste blood.

Whoever it was that coined that little sticks and stones phrase needed to be sticked and stoned.

It's quiet for a moment, and Kool and the Gang are doing their thing, the music down to a low audible. I've been repeating to myself that I really am *doing this*, really am driving across the state with a trunkful of stolen goods, partnering with a person that's a lot harder to be around than I thought. The song cuts into my thoughts as Jackie reaches over and turns the volume all the way up. "This is my jam, girl!" Though every sentence in my head is now a jumble, a toss-up of syllables and sounds, a single thought manages to make itself coherent: *I hardly know this woman.* Will she rat me out in some five years? Will I, her? Will there be other such missions? It all begins somewhere, one of those sociology experts would say.

The only image I have of the Hindenburg is from a quick blurb that NBC News ran seven or eight years ago, in 1988 or 1989, when the radio narrator of the disaster passed away. He became famous for his live coverage of the burning blimp, for his painful attempts to stay steady and professional while on the air, finally breaking down and sobbing *oh, the humanity . . . the humanity.* It was a snowy night in Albany, winter finals, and I remember looking up from my Spanish textbook at our black and white Zenith, listening to his teary voice, thinking about how much agony the passengers must have been in.

I left Albany in 1990 for Jersey State College via a volleyball scholarship but in my second semester fell in with Nick's father, which soon enough brought about Nick. This led to dropping out of college, only the first few steps in a long path of struggle and frustration. Unpaid bills. Estrangement from my parents. Working nickel-dime jobs.

How far does desperation have to take you? This far? We're parked at Fletcher's Gas-N-Go, and I'm watching Jackie through the large glass windows stuff items into the crook of her arm. A flashlight. Fig Newtons. Three Musketeers. A six of High-Life.

"You stay in the car and keep watch, girl," she told me when we first wheeled into the potholed parking lot. "I don't wanna lose two grand because we were too stupid to leave the goods unattended." There was something too-sure about her words that didn't set well. I wanted go inside, stretch my legs, scout around for my own snack. But *you stay*?

There was a night, maybe the third or fourth time I sat with Jackie at the bar, when this tone first surfaced. A social situation, an incident that both she and the bartender were rehashing, one that she summed up by bellowing out *I'll backhand that bitch if it happens*

13

again. She cackled at her own humor as the bartender grinned and poured her another drink, saloon-style. I was weary from a day of flirty contractors and invoices for Red Chief putty, and just wanted some like-minded company. But I took notice. Jackie, it seemed, wasn't scared of anything. I'm taking more notice now.

How far *does* desperation have to take you? Would I have to one day tell Nick how we afforded the move back to Albany? How Holly lost her mind and turned thief-for-an-eve, all for a thousand bucks?

We're back on the road, and Jackie's tapping her ring against the window, once again running her mouth. "I wonder if any of the Hindenburg's passengers had their fingers gripped to our cross-braces when the flames finally got to 'em."

I'm from New York. Was a college athlete. Became a single mother. So I'm not the softest gal around. But I can't believe the words I'm hearing.

"What do you think?" she says, looking for affirmation as she pops the top off her third High Life.

"I don't even know where a cross-brace *is* on a blimp," I say flatly.

She explodes in laughter, spitting flecks of beer across the front of the glove box. "What, and *I* do? Come on, girl, what do I know? I'm just a house painter. Hell, I don't even know how many people died

14

on the Hindenburg. But seriously, can you imagine? Some poor soul's hands plastered—no, *melted*—to the steel?! We outta tell this antique freak that they had to cut people's fingers from our braces just to remove their bodies. That way, we might be able to get another g out of him!"

She wraps all of this up with another burst of laughter and yet another big elbow to my side, slinging suds onto my shirt and lap.

We zip past a large cornfield, and in the deep distance the stars form a sprinkle of silver kernels that pock the backdrop of the night. I look at it but see very little. The idea that any human died while clinging to what we're about to profit from sickens me, even terrifies me; the news image of the Hindenburg going down in flames skips through my head, and the only thing able to drown it out is the endless howling from the woman to my right.

A boiling point. Did the Hindenburg have one of those? An instant where its hydrogen began to leak? A point at which the static electricity that danced around the balloon's periphery became too much, ripping into the airship's structure? A point of desperation?

Mine occurs at a Shamrock gas station. Tonight. May 17, 1996. 12:19 a.m. Somewhere in rural Jersey.

It happens but then, truth be told, I'm not exactly sure *what* happens.

For over half an hour Jackie's been yanking at my arm, telling me she's got to pee. So when the green roadside neon hits our sight she shrieks something idiotic and claps loudly, right outside my right eardrum. It's a run-down gas station, closed, not one of those all-night joints, so I pull around to the side and she stumbles out into the shadows and finds her way to a restroom that's no doubt seen the lowest of the lowest walks of life.

The passenger seat of my car is a train wreck. There's beer bottles and candy wrappers everywhere, and I, being the mother that I am, begin to scoop it all up in a fury, reaching over and stashing everything into Jackie's duffel bag. If she doesn't like it, to hell with her. I'm done with this drama.

But then it happens. I'm stuffing the last of Jackie's mess into the bag and there's this loud *clink*. I eye the bathroom door and decide to go for it, pulling the bag across the seat to my lap, wondering what in hell ol' girl's got in her dirty little bag. And there it is again. Not a glass on glass clink, but more like a glass on steel clink.

I rummage through a mess of towels and T-shirts, a pair of paint-splotched work boots. And there, right in front of me, lies a large grayish pistol. It's fantasy, something out of a detective show, but as real as the headache I've had for the last two hours. Starlight falls through the windshield, picking up the glint of the steel, the twinkle of the cold silver. I press the gears of my brain, frantic, scrambling to make a quick decision.

Was there a split moment when the Hindenburg's main captain could have made a difference? A few seconds where a lightning-like maneuver could have saved more lives? I'm told that some of us have such moments, a flicker of a crossroads in which the choice made will determine much of the rest of our life. For better. Or for worse.

I generally like my car clean. So off I go, coasting over the parking lot's broken asphalt, headed for the trash can I've just spotted. It's sitting at the pull-out to the main drag, right alongside a telephone booth. Through the glass I can see the juvenile scrawling all over the blue interior panel, *908-479-9219, Jake loves Sara!* and so on.

Window down, I reach over, begin discarding the trash from Jackie's little party. The Snickers wrappers are sticky, and the beer bottles feel warm and clammy in my hands; my knuckles nick the corner of Jackie's index card as I run my fingers through the crevices of the center console, collecting bottle caps, straw wrappers, other pieces of small trash.

Bag back on the floor, I sit still, the car still in park. The rearview mirror gives me a clean snapshot of the bathroom area. The bits of the blimp rest comfortably in the back. I'm teetering on the ledge of my own crossroads. Thinking about my future and my son. Wondering at just how sideways or right-ways life can become by a sudden snap decision.

I slide the car out of park, the engine of my mighty hooptie bracing for its next command. Is this how far desperation had to take me? I look in the rearview mirror again. I'm still not sure.

But then, maybe I am sure.

I'm sure that I'm better off *with* Jackie than away from her. That going for it could mean *asking for it.* The gear stick shifts smoothly into reverse.

I'm also sure how much better two grand is than one. That the gun that's only a few feet away probably means a lot more than I'm willing to entertain. That I simply can't take any of this anymore. The stick is now in drive, and it agrees with me. I mean, it really agrees with me.

But something that comes around every four or five days finds a way to happen at the worst possible moment: my Cutlass conks out, poof, lickety-split. The car rolls back gently as the engine goes dead, and I press the brake pedal and jam the engine into park. I grip the keys, about to re-start the ignition.

And there's Jackie, standing right at the passenger window, stooped over, staring at me.

Is this where desperation has finally dropped me off? Jackie opens the door, not taking her eyes off me.

I think I'm about to find out.

☛ 2

Pansy

Saying *nine over nine* is always kind of fun because painters are usually the only people that know what it means. The nine panes over nine panes in a large antebellum-style window represent a true challenge for a good brush-man on any job site. But if that newbie idiot in there doesn't stop saying it, or rather, howling it, then I'll have to make him. *The nine over nine's a switch in time . . .* is that what he's been singing? Dumb little nursery-rhyme-sissy. He wishes he could hold a candle to my brush-work. I've just finished the sashes around pane number seven, all coated in clean, white paint, glistening, not a speck on the glass. And boy am I fast.

See, now he's got me doing it. Skinny chump, in there rolling that bedroom out, trying to do it extra fast so Mark and the guys will think he's a first-class painter. It's Friday, only his third day and I'll give him a week, tops. I don't like pansy-men, walking around and singing on the job, that whole whistle-while-you-work attitude. And what the hell? Are those corduroys? Mark would never let us get away with something like that. Corduroys.

I pop a piece of Spearmint gum in my mouth, check my phone for any messages. Eleven dollars an hour isn't nearly enough to work this hard, and I have no qualms in taking my time when the moment arises. Mark throws me a few extra dollars every now and again, but he's doing pretty good, I'd say, and we're basically the reason for his success. We, yeah. Billy's upstairs manning the spray gun, Jerry's working the baseboards, and I'm on these windows. I don't count pansy boy as a legitimate asset on this team. No sir, weirdos, girlie-men, and dudes wearing corduroys on job sites need not apply.

You see, I've been grumpy all morning. Darlene's been complaining that her new three-thousand-dollar boob job makes her itch; Mark didn't have any coffee brewing this morning at the shop; and most of all, my bid wasn't accepted for that First National Bank paint job over on Commerce Boulevard in downtown Montgomery, the second bid I've recently lost. Big money, that job, and it was supposed to get me out of here, get me on to doing my own thing. It was also the kind of bread I needed since I'm the one making Darlene's extra payment every month. To top everything off—and something always does—the lady of the house, our customer, is walking around doing her daily chores in a pair of grey stretch pants. I've already dabbed more than one glob of paint on my wrist from being distracted and looking.

The crisp scent of cheese toast is dancing out of the kitchen, blending right in with the smell of exotic coffee, probably some of that fancy Columbian stuff percolating. I load up my brush with thick white paint and run it across the lower right-hand sash of the top window, listening to the low rumble of my empty stomach. *Nine over nine.* The bottom window's done, but I'm dragging. Unable to determine which is more aggravating: the succulent scent of the glory coming out of the kitchen or the sight of ol girl walking around in those pants. Her lower half looks like hammered steel underneath that thin layer of cotton. I wonder if her old man knows she's dressed like that around a bunch of painters. I suddenly get a good visual of her up on the kitchen table, dancing for us while we sit and watch while gulping that tasty coffee, all of us, Jerry, Billy, even sissy-man. The rumble in my stomach subsides and I feel a little better.

After a few minutes I can hear Madam Breakfast upstairs walking back and forth, doing something. But then there's movement in the kitchen. Nobody should be in the kitchen since we aren't painting in there, and so I lean my head back to get a view and I'll be damned if it ain't our resident goober himself, standing at the kitchen island, messing with something. I continue to watch, mortified with amusement, as he works his hand through a bowl of . . . cookies! He shoves one in his mouth, and after a quick check, left to right, he filches two more, stuffing them in his pocket. I duck my head back out of sight, wait for a second, and then lean back again to watch him re-work the pile of cookies, feathering them all out before stealing back to his room.

I turn back to my window and begin humming, *the nine over nine is a switch in time*. Now armed with a big grin, I plow through the next couple of panes, no longer bothered by the nagging smell of toast or coffee. Mark has hired a pickpocket! I work my brush cleanly up and down a sash, replaying what I've just seen. Is the newbie a thug in disguise? Maybe Mark hired him to watch us. Miss Lower-Half is now running down the stairs, probably having forgotten about her breakfast, and as I lean back and watch her breeze across the kitchen tile, she walks right past the cookie bowl and takes a cup out of the cabinet.

I return to my brush, wishing that I had it all on video. This is better than the movies.

***

The morning moves forward, and the latex is laid out with speed. Mark stops by with his daily check-in, making sure we've reached a certain point in our work. I'm in the little dining room breakfast nook, working through the windows when he pops his head around the kitchen door, looks across the room.

"You okay over there, Brooks?"

Earlier, I returned to my sulking, mulling over the lost bid and my financial situation, frowning because girlie-boy is now humming *zip-de-day-dooh-dah*, apparently his new tune. He's working in the living room, just around the corner, and I'm right annoyed with his happiness. I'm also angry at myself for telling Jerry about the lost bid because word could easily have gotten back to Mark. And since I didn't get that job I needed this one.

"Yeah, man," I say, sliding my wet Wooster brush across the dry, coarse sash of the center pane. "I'm good."

"You look like you missed your breakfast," he says, walking through the kitchen.

That's because you didn't have coffee for us this morning, the least you could do at the money we're making you. But I just bite my lip and keep on with the keeping-on. Mark and I are cool in general, but he's not big on sarcasm.

While Mark goes upstairs, I decide to move to the other window in the nook because the sun is blaring right through this one, and the glare off the white paint is excruciating. I can always come back later and finish it. I turn my body to face this new window, sliding my three-foot drop cloth under the sill and then whipping my old dust rag across the dry wood of the window's many corners and intricacies. Through the glass I look out at the front shrubbery and then over at another window that's a few yards down, set in the wall that runs the length of the living room. I'm distracted by an up-and-down motion through the sunny blur of the glass but it's soon clear that it's homer himself, rolling out the living room walls. His back is to me as he works.

A quick dip of my brush, a left-to-right pitter-pat on the insides of the bucket so the paint won't run down the sides of the bristles. That bank job was to have been the first in my new business, the jump-off for my own thing; it would have lasted at least two weeks, and the money would have been good. Lots of spraywork, brushwork, caulking, you name it. I've been painting for six years, right out of Montgomery Hills High School, and it's high time to get this show on the road. *Ain't never gonna make any money working for somebody else*, Dad always said, a little hometown homily I sometimes wish I'd never heard.

Pansy's right in my ten o'clock line of vision, and his corduroys and hat are a colorful blur through the glass and sashes and the holly bushes that run up against the side of the house. He starts the Mary Poppins routine again so I try to hone in and concentrate, put some of the panes under my belt. After all, Jerry is now working windows too, and there's always that unspoken race between painters, that subtle little contest between us roughnecks to see who can produce the most. More like who can work their ass off more for the same amount of money.

But what gives? Sugar-in-the-tank has come to a stop, his body going from the up-and-down motion to a kind of crouch. It looks as if he's kneeling in front of the television, sifting through something; it's hard to make out but I continue to squint through the two windows, the blood-red dots of the holly berries meshing right in with his red hat, all of it warped by the watery bend of the glass. I'm entranced by the dreamy visual

27

but finally decide to just peek around the corner of the nook and see what he's up to.

His back is to me but at a slight angle, and as he holds the roller pole over the bucket with his left hand, he picks through a box of cartridges and movies with his right. There's no mistaking the movie that he's checking out because it's the same one I just bought my father-in-law for his birthday: the twenty-fifth edition of *Raiders of the Lost Ark*, a golden-framed DVD with lost footage and interviews with the actors and producers. I'm looking right over his shoulder at the movie, and I'll be a monkey's uncle if Pansy doesn't check left to right, just as before, then crams the movie down into his pants. He remains crouched but quickly slides the bucket directly in front of him and begins to work the roller against the paint screen down in the bucket, getting it good and wet, pretending that he's been busy all the while, I gather, in case someone were to walk in.

I scootch back to my right and notice the globs of paint dripping down from my brush onto the red-brick tile of the floor. I grab my paint rag, mop it all up, and then take special notice of the many yet-to-be painted window sashes.

At least he snagged a good one. Raiders kicked ass, I always thought, right up there with *Rambo* and *Rocky*.

You come looking for Indy, you come looking for trouble. Pitter-pat, I load my Wooster up, and dive back into my work, way behind. Yeah, he got something worthy. If the new guy had taken something like *Titanic* or Hugh Grant, I'd have to lose complete respect for him.

***

Lunch always tastes good when someone else pays for it, even if it is at Mawmaw's, the stickiest barbecue joint in central Alabama. Jerry finally made good on the lunch he owed me from months ago. As we shuffle through the blistering parking lot back to the jobsite, letting the grease seep into our system, I glance over at him. Jerry's a big, burly fellow in his fifties, looks a lot like Burl Ives, and was probably born with a brush in his hand.

"What do you make of the new guy?" I finally ask. Since Pansy went to lunch with Billy I wanted to take advantage of the opportunity.

He doesn't look at me but just keeps on walking. "I try not to."

We trudge on through the lot of the outdated Piggly Wiggly, which sits just behind the subdivision where we're working. A tow truck zips by, pulling a rusted-out Volkswagen, and the summer humidity grips us like a body cast.

"Why?" Jerry offers. "He creep you out a little?"

"I wouldn't put it that way. He's weird, all right."

"Yep." He fishes a fresh pack of Pall Malls out of his back pocket and does the tap-the-end routine. "That all?"

I give it some more thought and decide to let it go. I'm not sure Jerry would even believe me. Pansy doesn't fit the thief type, and something about it just makes me want to see it play out. As we walk through the heat back to our labor, Jerry exhales a thick blast of cigarette smoke which hovers over us like a dust cloud over Pig-Pen.

"Brooks, is that all you've done today?"

Billy is standing in the breakfast nook, pointing at the windows, tugging at his green bandana that's pinning down a mass of bushy, blonde hair. Here we go with the comparisons, with the typical *show me what you've done* that I get tired of hearing.

"Come on, man," he says, shaking his head. "You've got to step it up a little."

"I did the windows in the foyer too," I say weakly, pointing to the front door area, knowing that it's not a lot to fall back on. But it's all I have.

"Ramp it up some, chief," he says over his shoulder as he jogs back upstairs. "We gotta finish this job."

Jerry's walking back to wherever he was working, but I know he's listening. Candy ass—I just realize I don't even know his name—has just walked in and is also headed back to his post but I know he's getting an earful as well.

I didn't like being called out in front of the guys like that, even if it was over something minor, so I take my time getting back to work. Besides, I've gone beyond the minimum on plenty of other jobs. And if I'd gotten that bank job I wouldn't be dealing with all this, I keep telling myself.

Mawmaw's sweet tea is working its way through my system, so I walk to the bathroom. After doing my thing, I wash my hands and dry off, looking at all the ridiculous lotions on the counter, letting my mind wander. A colorful mobile hanging above catches my eye, a handful of thongs hang-drying. Red, purple, black, just like that. The visual of Honey-Bottom dancing on the table—this time in one of those bright thongs I'm currently studying—comes back to me, and Billy's little lecture is gone for now.

This bathroom is way at the other end of the house, and it leads right out into a small hallway with dark flooring that runs right past the boy's bedroom. There's no light on and as I walk out my foot bumps against something soft and bulky; my eyes adjust to the dim light and I see that I've kicked over Pansy's backpack. He's apparently draped a large T-shirt over the bag, and as I reach down to straighten everything I look into the open backpack. And I see something.

I pause, not hearing anything or anybody in this part of the house, and then quickly reach into the bag and pull it out, something plastic and detailed, something— thanks to the comics that I collected as a kid—that I instantly recognize. It's Green Arrow, a tall, vintage figurine, maybe a foot high, and I know right away that our pickpocket is at it again.

I'm freaked out yet fascinated by his choice of things to steal. Cookies. A DvD. A kid's toy collectable?

I stash the figurine back into the backpack and can now hear Pansy in the boy's bedroom, working the roller. I stop at the door and watch him for a moment, his back to me once again. The kid's room is that of a typical ten-year-old you'd find anywhere: posters of dinosaurs and Star Wars, soccer balls under the bed, a large Auburn University banner hanging from the ceiling. A shelf high up over the bed contains the rest of the super hero figurines, neatly lined up. Aquaman, Superman, Captain Cold, Flash, others I didn't recognize. As I slip away I glance at the top of the room's dresser, which is covered with stacks and stacks of little bags of Reese's Pieces. I've never seen so much candy in one setting and figure they must be for a candy drive or for school. Baseball, or maybe Boy Scouts.

***

Sometime after three or so I've got my afternoon wind. I'm blowing through the inside of the closet trim in the master bedroom, whistling some beer commercial that's been in my head since hearing it at lunch. I've got plastic drop cloths all around because there's a mountain of shoes on the closet floor. Jerry's over there working the inside trim to the bedroom's largest window. He's got his own problems. Since we're only painting the trim in the bedrooms, we opted to not take down the curtains and everything. But it's a decision we're now not crazy about. Hot pants has one of those ridiculous oversized curtain arrangements hanging down in front of the window, and Jerry has to hold back part of the curtain just to maneuver his brush up inside the window frame to work. All you can see is the shape of his big head and shoulders inside the curtain, poking around, and I have to fight back a laugh.

After a few minutes I hear the door click followed by the low rumbling of a voice. After peering out from my little cave, I see Billy standing there, upset over something.

"At lunch, that sumbitch walked right out of Rhonda's without payin'!" Though Billy's voice is down to a husky murmur I can hear him clearly. "I couldn't believe it," he goes on, excited. "He just walked out."

Jerry's head and shoulders are sticking out from the dark red drapery, and he looks like a confused king. "No kidding. What did he say?"

"He giggled like a little girl about it! He just says, 'Watch this,' and you know how there's always a crowd up around the register, and not really a line?"

Jerry nods. "My wife's been telling Rhonda for years to change that little format. Ain't never worked."

"Well, he just strolled up to the front, through all the customers, and walked right out. They had that Friday special goin' so it was real crowded. He even offered to pay for half my check once he met me outside."

"You take it?"

"Course I didn't take it! I don't want no part of that." The more Billy talks, the more upset he becomes. He checks the door, presumably to make sure nobody can hear him, and then he pulls off his dirty bandana, running his caulk-crusted fingertips through his rough mop of hair. I still don't think he's seen me so I remain still.

Jerry stands there, shaking his head, but remaining as calm as ever. You could tell Jerry there was a nationwide ban on cigarettes and that they were cancelling *This Old House* and he'd have the same, relaxed demeanor. "Poor Rhonda's been dined and dashed on a lot over the years," he says. "All those damn college kids from Alabama State do it. I once heard my neighbor's kids talking about it out in the driveway, bragging about it. Just ain't right."

"Need to do something," Billy says. "Don't we? This can't just go by and be forgotten."

I'm sitting there, locked into his words. Billy, the elder statesman of our paint crew, angry and aggravated. I'm thinking I should stand up and offer my two cents but now he's talking again. "Yep. We gotta do something."

"Well," Jerry says with a slow nod. "It wouldn't hurt."

"We just can't let it go. This is —"

"What if he just forgot?" I say, going for it, poking my head around the corner of the closet. I don't want to give Billy any chance to act surprised or ask why I didn't speak up sooner so I keep on. "That does happen. People sometimes do that."

They're staring a hole right through me so I keep up whatever it is I'm doing. "People, you know, get confused and walk out without paying sometimes."

"Brooks," Billy says, as if talking to a toddler. "He *laughed* about it outside. He didn't forget. What are you talkin' about?" I'm watching Jerry's granite-like expression as Billy talks, but then there's a voice right at the door, followed by a quick knock.

"Uh, guys? Are you in here?" It's the lady of the house, asking if one of us can move our car to let her out.

"Yeah, that's my car," offers Billy, forcing a quick smile at her at her through the half-opened door. "Be right there." He turns to leave but shoots me the strangest look he's ever given me as he walks out, slowly twirling his bandana.

I skate down the last three-foot stretch of the closet trim, brushing out any remaining runs or buildup of paint. Jerry's head is back inside the big window outfit. Before he has a chance to say anything about my odd concern for the new guy, I put my brush down in the pot, crawl out into the room, and walk out to the garage.

I've got the four o'clock cottonmouth so I grab a Dr. Pepper from our work cooler. I stand in the driveway, in the shade of the mammoth oak trees all around, drinking my soda and trying to piece together the lyrics to that beer commercial. I concentrate on the cinder-block back of the Piggly Wiggly building, and then my eyes catch Billy, who's sitting in his car in a new parking space out front, talking on his cell, still playing with his bandana.

I throw back my Dr. Pepper and finish it off. Soon we'll be done with this job and then on to the next. And I'm thinking about how long I'll be with this little paint company, doing this kind of work. In fact, I'm thinking about a lot of things.

****

Later, on the drive home, I stuff my face with Reese's Pieces. An evening wind blows through the central Alabama dusk, kicking up the ubiquitous scent of paint that's become part and parcel of my old work van. The traffic is not too bad, and the beautiful pockets of black and purple stretching across the horizon bring to mind one of Honey-Bottom's thongs, which was coiled up like a coral snake inside my work bag, stuffed away in a large Ziploc bag I slipped out of the kitchen when nobody was around. A little five-fingering, yes-sir, never hurt anybody. Unless you are too stupid not to know when to stop.

I fish another bag of Reese's from the large pile on my passenger seat, tear off the top of the plastic with my teeth, and think about the patrol car parked out in front of Mark's shop after work. When we first returned to the shop I'd wondered if it was just one of Mark's weekend running buddies, since it was Friday afternoon. But my instincts told me the car was there for something else. Which, we found out, it was.

A fresh box of caulk and a handful of putty knives—things to avenge our departed friend—lay comfortably in the back of my van, a mere drop in the bucket when you consider the size of Mark's stock. My new acquisitions could be the first step back in the direction of my new business and my next bid. The second step just might be those lonely power tools lying in the bed of neighbor Carl's truck I've lately been paying some mind to. Tools like that, left out in the wide open, are just asking for a better home.

Although our paint crew will now be without Mr. Pansy, there will be honor among thieves, at least on this particular Friday evening. I'll think of you, sir, when I get things going. When I'm running my own crew, and am knocking down jobs left and right. Yessir, a customer's oatmeal cookies, as we're caulking that kitchen door jamb, will taste just right, and make the grunt of the workday worthwhile. A juice box from the pantry to wash everything down. A little gift here, a little gift there, done with just the right balance. The beer commercial has left my memory and I'm now back to humming the melody that began the day. *The nine over nine's like a switch in time.* See ya on the other side, amigo.

☛3

Burn the Demons Out

Dewey was the only person who could ever relate to my *Amityville Horror* experience. The only person. It was one of those Sunday night movies—not on cable but regular prime-time television, the kind that everyone else I knew had. And there I was, home alone, 1980, unable to look away from that big, looming house lit up by towering shards of lightning, all of it enhanced by creepy music as the credits unfolded. What in the world . . .? Like most bizarre things that you can't believe you're witnessing, I was unable to look away.

"Sidney, did you watch that creepy crap last night?" Dewey asked the next day. "The American horror show? About that haunted house?" We were getting our morning math work ready.

"*The Amityville Horror*," I corrected him. "I watched it. It gave me nightmares."

"I would have saved you from them if I could have come over," he said, popping me in the arm with his Wacky Package folder. I laughed and quickly looked down, making sure my sleeves were pulled down over my skin good and snug so my arms wouldn't look fat.

Even in the fifth grade there was always a little more to our friendship than met the eye. There was Dewey, whispering *Montgomery* across the aisle to me during our test on state capitals; there I went, slipping him my extra stamps during the book fair so he could purchase a cool pack of Halloween pencils. And later in the schoolyard, he told me he would protect me. "I'll pour gasoline all over the front porch," he screamed from atop the monkey bars, his tiny black curls damp with perspiration. "And then light a match and burn the demons out!"

As a kid, he always had a knack for pomp and bravado, and liked to display it. But here we were, adults—or something that resembled it—approaching forty, trying to ready ourselves for the approaching sludge of middle age. And now it was me doing the protecting.

"Are you still going to try and burn the demons out?" I asked him over his shoulder as he paid for our banana malts. The teenage girl behind the counter handed back the change and gave us a quick peek, probably trying to size up our relationship. As if anybody could ever size up our relationship. Was she looking at me, this tattooed adolescent, wondering just what business this chubby woman had in sucking down a large malt? We walked out, an old cowbell clanging against the glass door of one of Long Island's forgotten sixties-style burger stands. And I gave her the look I once gave one of the skinny young reporters at my first job at WAJD in Phoenix after she told me she was going to be the head anchor within five years.

"Did I tell you that?" Dewey asked as he climbed in and revved up the engine of the Ford rental to get the heater warm. "That sounds like something I would have said." It was March, and still chilly in New York.

"You did. In the schoolyard one day."

"Yeah, I remember. Vaguely. Dang, we just met up and you're already playing the memory game."

I picked up the map from the center console as he veered the truck back out onto the street. "Please. Every time you text me you bring up one of our misadventures."

"The misadventures of Dewey and Sidney," he said, looking over at me, grinning. "Does that include going out and getting high?"

"How could it not include that?"

"Make you a deal," he said. Though they had filled out even more with time, his round, full cheeks still had that boyish glisten, even at night. "Keep talking to Will's brother for me. Uh, what's his name?"

"Brian."

"Brian. Keep talking to Brian for me and, sure, I'll burn those demons out. Hell, I'll burn the whole damn house down." The birthmark on his neck was the size of my pinkie, long and slender, forever a deep purple against his coffee-colored skin. But it now looked black. Did those things change with age?

The house at 112 Ocean Ave, Amityville was something we'd talked about visiting the minute we both wound up in the New York area at the same time. And that day had finally arrived: me in Queens, on a week-long assignment with my crew from Milwaukee's WXVO, Dewey in Jersey City, attending his cousin's wedding. It was Saturday night, and we'd met up for lobster and drinks, gushing over the previous year or so since we'd last seen each other. "Job going okay?" I asked after we ordered, to which he just sort of nodded with a strange smirk. Dewey worked as head of security at a small bank in Fremont, back where we grew up; but in recent years boredom had crept in, and he ceased to talk about his work or display any interest.

He usually had a fiery interest in my career as a broadcast journalist, asking about the latest network where I was working, how far I'd advanced. But after dinner, when we hopped into his rental and began driving out to Long Island, it was clear there was one thing he wanted to talk about. I'd been dating Will for about a year and had recently met his brother Brian, who had fourteen years with the Border Patrol. And ever since I told Dewey what Brian did for a living he constantly asked about it in his emails and text messages. Tonight was turning out to be no different.

"Turn left at Paddington," I said, squinting hard at the map, trying not to sound like I was changing the subject. There were at least three streets named 'Ocean' in the area, and it was frustrating. Neither of us wanted to be the weirdo tourist, stopping and asking for the location of one of Long Island's sickest crimes.

"So you never answered my last email. Have you talked to Brian lately? At all?"

"No, not since Thanksgiving," I began. "Not really, anyway. I told you that, right? He sent me and Will a few of those dumb spam jokes, and that was pretty much it. He did say that, you know, you can always apply again once a full year has passed." Brian had considerable experience in recruiting and hiring new candidates. I didn't want to say that he'd told me the Border Patrol had in recent years drastically altered its hiring policy.

"Okay, so you did talk to him at Thanksgiving. Good." Dewey looked over at me curiously, and then out at the houses slowly passing by. "You were kind of vague about that in your e-mails."

"Well, yeah, I thought I told you that I talked to him then. We just didn't talk a lot," I said, lying. "Not a whole lot anyway. You know how the holidays are, with everybody gabbing at the same time."

"I don't see why the whole thing's taking so long. I applied with them nine months ago. I mean, it's not like it's the CIA or anything. It's the Border Patrol."

I made sure our eyes met. "You know that Brian is in a different quadrant now, right? He really has no influence in the hiring process anymore."

"I know, I know, I know." Dewey spoke quickly, a kind of high whine to his voice. "You told me. Sorry,

I'm just impatient. I know he can't really do anything. I'd just kind of like his insight."

I pointed to the next street and motioned for him to turn, checking the map to make sure I was right. "Dewey, he's just really busy. And I don't know him that well. I've only been around him twice. Once for their uncle's fiftieth-year anniversary thing. And then Thanksgiving."

He didn't say anything and I smoothed my right hand down over my jacket so that it covered all of my lap. All it takes is a banana malt to destroy the momentum and confidence of a diet.

"Besides," I continued, "I just wouldn't feel that comfortable trying to find out stuff like that from Will's brother. You know?" He grunted and nodded, and I turned my attention back to the window, searching for a street address on any of the houses.

The neighborhoods we were driving through could basically pass for the same neighborhoods of any other part of the country. But now, the houses increasingly looked older, even larger, and the surrounding trees and foliage turned darker and fuller, more mature. Though I was unsure about where the conversation was headed, I was becoming giddy with the fifth grade spooks and chills once again. When Dewey said something cynical about Will I cut him off and quickly pointed to a house that seemed familiar.

"Hey, this looks just like that house that we crashed out near Berkeley. That dumb frat party. Remember?" A big tire swing hung from a massive oak tree in the front yard, and the old house boasted one of those antebellum-style wrap-around front porches.

"Gosh," he said. "Maybe. Wasn't that down in San Jose? There were so many nights like that."

"Remember? That huge tire swing and those silly-looking gargoyle statues they had out front?" I felt stupid even asking because I knew he'd forgotten a lot of those houses. They say that marijuana affects everybody in different ways but memory loss wasn't something I was ready to accept. Not just yet.

I moved on, knowing there would be victory in other recollections. "You *do* remember the nights out at that haunted pier, right? When we jumped in the water and stirred up all those frogs? All that loud croaking?"

"Of course," he said, with a retort, suddenly tapping the accelerator, which jerked the truck forward a bit. "Why wouldn't I remember that? That was classic."

I checked the map again, and realized we'd passed our street. There was another house with a large wraparound porch; a trio of sugar maple trees filled most of the yard, and on top of a giant pile of leaves lay a red rake.

"Are they close?" he asked. "Those two?"

When I turned to him he was scratching his birthmark, which seemed even darker. "Who? Will and Brian?"

"Yeah."

"No, not really. I don't know."

He focused on the road and I studied his birthmark, telling myself that now was the time to stop the charade. Trying to play nice and ignorant was only doing harm. "Well, actually," I said, "they *are* rather close, come to think of it. Hey, turn around up here. We were supposed to make a left back there. You missed it."

He got the car turned around but clicked his tongue all the while, not saying anything; I could almost hear him concentrating. "Do you think that maybe . . . maybe it's because I'm mixed?" he said. "I mean, I *am* a minority."

Though it was rare, Dewey had tried this angle a few times in the past; it usually happened in college when he failed a class. He'd call me up and go on and on about how he'd studied so hard the night before the final exam, how he deserved to pass the class. *Can you believe it? I never thought that teacher liked me, anyway. Maybe she's a bigot.*

"Dewey, come on. It's a different world. The president is mixed."

"Well, I'm just wondering. Maybe that's why the Border Patrol hasn't contacted me yet. Right?"

"I guess so." I checked our map again, making sure we were on the right street. "I guess anything's possible." I had my own experiences with discrimination, or at least something akin to it, and really didn't want to hear his. Lead anchor for WCBV in Phoenix. Lead anchor for WXCR in San Jose, and then WCNJ in Sacramento. All of them had gone to other television journalists. Younger, thinner journalists.

"I bet Will wouldn't bring you out here," he said.

I smiled and shook my head. He was right on that. Will spooked easily, almost too easily, I sometimes thought. I don't think he'd even seen the *Amityville Horror*. Dewey and I, shoot, we'd watched it—along with other horror films—many times over. In middle school, high school, and then in our college years when he came home on weekends. *Salem's Lot, Child's Play, The Omen.* Scary stuff was what we did. We'd be on the floor, Dewey giving me a massage while someone's throat was being sliced open ear to ear. Later, we'd smoke a joint while Dewey talked about how annoying his latest girlfriend was, or how the local FBI affiliate had declined his internship application. To hell with them, though, he said. He would one day arrest people that counterfeited money or sold drugs. After college. After he got all of the partying and the pot out of his system.

We exchanged postcards in those years, met up for the occasional long weekend, hung out during the holidays. Time trickled by and we were apart more often, but our communication remained consistent, the phone calls and letters eventually morphing into emails and text messaging. Yet our relationship never really got out of the starting blocks. We were too much like siblings. There was Dewey, handing me my Dukes of Hazzard lunchbox as we came in from recess, then running off to lead his club of rowdy boys, the Silver Eagles. There he was, punching out Donnie Remick in the eighth grade for calling him a chubby chaser but then only a few short months later taking Lisa McKenzie to the prom. There were the two of us on graduation day, taking a picture with the whole class, holding hands and hugging, his birthmark beautifully mirroring the dark purple tones of our caps and gowns.

And now here we were, in that pocket of life that falls right before the looming years of middle age, dating other people, living here and there. Dewey chasing his fading dream of becoming a federal agent, me clawing my way through thirteen years of broadcast journalism, always settling for the role of backup anchor. Fighting with the fact that most news stations rarely opted for aging, heavy-set candidates when selecting a lead anchor.

"So you already know about my dull job. Nothing new there. How's it going in Milwaukee?" he asked. "You've never really told me. Do you ever get spotted out in public?"

I ran my fingers across the collar of my jacket, pondering whether or not to go into my latest career complaints. But then there was a sudden thrust of the Long Island breeze through the cab, the cool air swimming all around, and Dewey was exultant with something.

"Sidney? Do you see it?"

I looked up from the map and *did* see it. Out of nowhere the street had become even darker, the wind quicker, gustier, and the house, despite some minor renovations, looked the same as it had on television. It sat there, bold and shadowy, powerful. And for the moment, Brian and the Border Patrol and everything else were gone.

"That's it," Dewey whispered, letting the truck coast, the happy horror of elementary school encircling us. I seized his hand, feeling a frenzy of memories as I looked out at the long, thin chimney snaking up between the two eye-like windows on either side. The house was huge, was *still* huge, sitting just behind a series of thick elms and sycamores. And suddenly I was lying on the orange shag carpet in my living room back in Fremont. A Sunday night, alone with our twelve-inch black-and-white Zenith and my imagination. Locked into some disturbing movie that CBS executives never should have allowed on the air.

"That's it," he repeated, soft and scratchy, and the wind shot through the cab, blowing his dark locks across his forehead. He squeezed my palm while maneuvering the truck slowly past the house and then carefully around the loop of the cul de sac. There was a quick, kinetic jolt to our handholding, further warmed by the spook and the thrill of the moment. For now, the obstacles in our professional lives, the potential specter of discrimination, didn't amount to a hill of beans. And though I knew that the house was harmless, I still needed Dewey here beside me.

Our rental slowly sauntered by one more time, past the last of the corner shrubbery, and we looked back for one final peek at the looming mansion, at the dark clapboard siding that surrounded those eerie windows that I'd give anything to look through. I was enraptured, free-falling through the days of Fremont's Adelia Williams elementary school. Flitting through the wonderful childhood of me and Dewey, of those creepy, comfortable nights watching Damian Omen and Chucky. And I refused to re-enter the ubiquitous monotony of Long Island and its surroundings.

But we were slapped back into this reality, driving past a Roy Rogers restaurant, then an Army recruiting station. Dewey had both hands on the wheel and was chatting away like a ten-year-old.

"Did you see that? Can you believe someone actually lives there? They must have gutted the whole inside and started from scratch!"

He shrieked loudly with glee, and then clapped his hands together. "Damn! Sidney, when I'm finally working for the government and carrying a concealed weapon, I'll come back here and make that house look like Swiss cheese!" He clapped again, louder, as if to cap the whole thing off.

Clapping, just like he did back in grade school, high up on those monkey bars. Demonstrating with both hands how he'd pour gasoline over the house's front porch and then light a match, *burning the demons out!* Dewey, magnificent and confident, towering over the rest of us in the schoolyard.

Animated, just like when I'd driven up to Sacramento to see him during college for a Labor Day barbeque. He was gabbing away, his arm over the small of my back so I wouldn't back into the hot grill, relaying to his fraternity brothers a fishing trip we'd taken years before. He rambled his way on to surmising over his eventual employment with the FBI or CIA. He was always exuberant in his stories and predictions.

Protective, that was Dewey the night of his twenty-eighth birthday. He was in Fremont after finally graduating college, and we celebrated by breaking into crybaby house, an old abandoned mansion across town responsible for more than one urban legend. We were with a small group of friends from high school, and as we climbed the creaky staircase, the women shushing the men to keep quiet, Dewey turned to me with a muffled giggle. The scent of warm pot was all over his breath. "You know, you shouldn't be next to me. Black men are always the first to go in places like this." We arrived on the landing, stepping through the thick cobwebs and dust, and he pulled me in closer to him, still laughing. "Come on, let's catch up. They're gonna smoke one in the room where the baby supposedly died."

"Sidney, are you listening?"

He'd been talking about something.

"Huh? Oh. What?"

"I asked you why you didn't get a picture."

"Oh. Uh. I didn't even think about it. Better for posterity, no? We'll have to rely on our memories."

He looked at me with a nod and his quick smile, the mesh of neon, bricks, and trees zipping by behind him out the window. For a moment I watched the wind rip through his hair, seeing for the first time the thirty-eight-year-old man that he'd become.

"Dewey?"

"Yeah? What's up?"

I powered my window up, the strong swaths of the evening breeze a little too much. I quickly decided any further talk on the subject could wait.

"Sid, what is it?"

"I . . . I was just going to ask if we had enough gasoline."

"Gas? Of course, goofy. Got over half a tank left."

Now wasn't the time to tell Dewey what I did or didn't know. Maybe later. Maybe tomorrow. But not now. There had been other words exchanged between me and Brian, many more words. But for the moment,

Dewey's problems and obstructions—for that matter, *our* problems and obstructions—were fading, thinning into the sprawling New York night. And although I remained silent, I knew: the day had finally arrived in which I would no longer protect him from the truth.

"Come on, let's head back," he said. "I checked the cable schedule at the hotel before I left. *Cujo* is on at midnight, and I don't want to miss it." His smile was big and broad, and I could now tell: his birthmark *was* black. He squeezed my hand again, and the truck picked up acceleration as he navigated it back out onto Sunrise Highway.

We were quiet as the creep of Amityville sailed through our minds and the night, all of the horror that went down in that hapless house during the summer of 1975, the way it had blossomed into part of our popular culture. We exited Sunrise Highway and fell right into the craze of the 495. The sudden visual of Dewey and his government-issued handgun made me grin. He was right there in the front yard, spraying holes in that clapboard siding, picking off the ghosts in the upstairs windows. The majesty and the fright of the evening took precedence over all else, and for now the bond of comfort, contentment, and discovery that we shared would suffice.

4

Holly and Cobb's Cleats

There they sit, two tattered pairs of baseball spikes attached to the inside of a mahogany case lidded in glass. As I stand here, they're the only thing that have my attention. For the last fifteen minutes, my aunt Blanche has been inside, frantically searching for our never-mailed Christmas card, and she insisted that Nick and I not leave without it. But right now, it's all about the spikes. They're at the rear of the neighbor's station wagon, crammed in alongside all sorts of other boxes and baseball paraphernalia. Bats, gloves, old uniforms, small glass cases, each displaying the ball that was hit breaking a particular record. A big purple and white cardboard placard stuffed against a window, *Welcome 1993 Inductees*, even though the year is 1997. The afternoon heat of New York is dive-bombing in, catching the top of the glass, a kamikaze of glass and sun.

The only reason we're here is that aunt Blanche's home is one exit down from Winky's Waterpark—which is where we've been all day—and Dad's been pressuring me to drop in when I'm in the area and let her see Nick. But today, dropping in on my great aunt has also meant dropping in on her nerdy neighbor. Since we arrived, she's been walking back and forth between her house and car, carrying armloads of base-ball knick-knacks, gabbing away about her twenty-four years at Cooperstown, then gushing over the busted water main that flooded the museum's basement just a few days ago.

"I volunteered to take care of some of this stuff while they cleaned everything up," she said, while hauling a glass case full of old-timey gloves. "But now I've got to get it all back to the museum!"

She's got that exaggerated seriousness about her, and since she and Blanche share the big dual driveway between their homes, I've been standing here, hostage to her yakking. Nick, my quirky son, is over in the backyard, trying to jump up and catch dragonflies. The things that go on in a nine-year-old's mind.

Back to the shoes. I'm trying to be a good girl. We did our duty. Sat down to a plate of stale Ritz crackers, some knock-off ginger ale. Listened to Blanche's daily medication routine while staring at floral-print peach wallpaper from yesteryear. It's time to get this silly holiday card, collect my son, and skidaddle. But given the status of my checking account, the shoes have made things very interesting. And when I think back to one particular antique dealer in rural New Jersey, the situation has gone from interesting to downright fascinating. *If you ever come across any old baseball items bring 'em in. I usually give a pretty penny for that stuff.* I'm paraphrasing but you get the idea.

Does being broke ever become, well, *hip*? Fashionable? To me, it's as normal as getting out of bed or staring at a billboard on the highway. When you get right down to it, Winky's was a luxury that we really couldn't afford. One of those the-bills-be-damned situations, the kind you regret the second you drive away, the fun of the day fading. I shift my weight from left to right, look over at the ragged tarp folded up under a rusted toolbox in the back of my old Cheyenne pickup. A plan's developing in my head. The hot summer air is empty of noise, save the jumping about of Nick, who's moved down to the other end of Aunt Blanche's back-yard. He's now engaged in some kind of conversation with the dragonflies.

Across the pavement, through the screened window, I've got a clear visual of my aunt, her arms and head still buried in a large box, sifting away. I swivel to my right, glance at the side door of the neighbor's house. Nothing. And then, as quickly as Winky's took our twenty dollars entrance fee, I walk to the back door of the station wagon. Give the spikes another good gander. And then do the deed.

Here's the tricky part: trying to explain to my unpredictable son the sudden reason for the two to three hour drive to Jersey. But since we live in Grand Gorge, and have driven a good forty-five minutes south to get to Winky's, we're generally already going in the right direction. As we hit the road I seize upon part of our earlier conversation with aunt Blanche and manage to pull it off.

"I may never get to see Ruthie again, Nick. She lives in Hainesville, and we're now only a couple of hours away. It'd be a shame if we didn't pay her a visit."

"Tonight? Right now?"

"You heard us talking about her, didn't you? In aunt Blanche's kitchen?"

"I heard something about somebody being sick. But I—"

"That was her. Ruthie. She has leukemia. I don't know when we'll be this close to her again. She'd love a surprise visit."

All of this is not a total fib since there actually is a Ruthie, a third cousin twice removed or some such, somewhere in New Jersey. It's just that I'm having the hardest time remembering what she looks like. A dark violet haze drops across the horizon as we drive. Nighttime isn't far off, and I'm slowly trying to piece together the time frame between now and our destination.

"So what do you say, son? It's the weekend so why not?" I check for his reaction but he just twinkles his eyes and quickly nods, now rocking back and forth to R.E.M on his headphones. He's thinking that we'll soon be driving through the city, taking in the spectacular view that the Queensborough Bridge affords; at least, that's what I believe he's thinking. Truth is, I seldom know what he's thinking.

I should probably be more nervous than I am since I've no clue if my contact is still in business, or even still with us. In fact, I wouldn't know where else to go with two pairs of old baseball cleats. Frank's an old-timer, one of those antique oddballs who sometimes

61

sells but always collects. At the McDonald's down the road, I pull over and fish his crinkled phone number—still there!—from the tiny zippered pouch inside my purse. I'm at the pay phone while Nick runs around the playground, frequently stopping to give Ronald McDonald a massage, which is a disturbing visual. But now *I'm* disturbed since nobody's answering. I hang up, shove the change back into the slot and dial again, panic setting in. But then someone picks up, a growlish voice that sounds about a million miles away.

"Um. Is this Frank?"

"Depends on who wants to know."

I summon a big breath and take my time. "Well. I did some business with you three or four years ago. You probably remember . . . buying some rare parts from that famous blimp? The Hindenburg?" That's a story in itself but it's neither here nor there. A long pause.

"Cross braces. Yep, I recall. Tall, blond gal? Came out here in the middle of the night?"

"Yes. I've got something else, something historic you might have an interest in." There's another huge pause before he speaks, and so I turn to check on Nick, who's now up on the shoulders of Ronald, piggyback style.

"I'm listening," he finally says.

I begin with the details and it's as if I do this all the time, the ease and the comfort setting in as I speak, the ickiest of sensations. *What in hell is this ..?*

It's a pair of new shoes for my son. That's what it is. It'll mean steak and lemon pie, instead of TV dinners and Jello. It could also mean paying my parents back the money I borrowed over a year ago. Since becoming a mother, I've never been intimate with the notion of 'financially getting ahead' and I'd like to end that drought.

"*The* Ty Cobb?" he asks.

"Yep." I assumed there weren't two Ty Cobbs.

"They're still in the wooden case, with the official Cooperstown stamp?"

"Uh-huh."

"In decent shape, you say? With his name on the inside? Is it legible?"

"It's right on the inside heel of the cleat. At the top, in thick red ink."

"Come on, then. I close early on Saturdays but just ring that outside bell and I'll let you in through that side door. Same as you did last time. You remember?"

"I remember."

He gives me a ballpark on what he can pay me, and after quickly jotting down directions, we're back on the road, headed for Jersey. Headed for God knows what.

***

7:10 p.m. Newburgh, New York. We hit a slight dip on the 87, and after hearing the box slide across the grooves of the bed I turn and steal a peek through the window, see that it's moved a few feet out from the edge of the tarp. Just one more time, I reiterate to myself. Cobb's cleats won't bring anything like the two grand the Hindenburg pieces brought but that's okay. I'm no common crook. Just gonna cash this little piece of baseball history in and that'll be it. I take another quick look, making sure the shoes haven't moved again but then there's a wet sensation creeping alongside my right hip, now on to my ass. I look down at the jumbo cup of iced Grapico that's spilled over the seat.

"Nick!" I shriek. "Look at what you've done!"

He yanks off his headphones and looks down at the mess, which is mostly on my side of the seat. "Sorry, mama," he says, grabbing the few napkins I have stashed in the glove box. "The drink was propped up and I guess I forgot about it."

I remember the knockoff Yankees jersey I once stuffed under the seat—a rookie named Darran Jeter or something or the other—and I pull the truck off onto the shoulder.

"What are you doing?"

"What does it look like, son?" I snap, jumping out and digging around for the shirt. "You made one hell of a mess." After locating it, I press the shirt down into the seat cushion, soaking up whatever I can. Nick brushes the ice off onto the ground and helps me dab the seat with the jersey. The evening traffic roars by, big cars, small cars, an eighteen-wheeler hot on the wheels of a grey Amigo.

"Well," he says, "maybe somebody or something is trying to tell us that going to New Jersey so late is a mistake."

I look across the seat at him and don't say anything. Nick's never had a difficult time expressing himself and so he continues. "Right? I mean, who is this cousin again?"

We climb back in and begin easing out on the highway. In the rear-view distance a white blur of oncoming headlights is coming on quick so I mash the gas, the tires squealing into the night.

"Her name is Ruthie. I told you, she's my second cousin. On grandma Lana's side."

He just sits there, staring through the windshield.

"I haven't seen her in forever, since you were very little. I just thought it'd be a nice little road trip. She's only a few hours away, and she told me on the phone she'd love to see us."

We shoot by a Coors Light billboard, a gang of air-headed blondes holding beer bottles, smiles and breasts all over the place. I fix my focus on the taillights ahead of us, inching our speed up to seventy-five. The less said, the better. I know that Nick will be out like a light come nine, nine-thirty at the latest. He's never had trouble falling asleep in the truck, and the consistency of his heavy sleeping patterns is one of the few predictable things about him.

"Ruthie, huh?" he finally mumbles. "Yeah, I think I remember hearing her name from you or grandma, a long time ago."

"She's only in her fifties but she's been really ill. And I figured this might be one of the last times I get to see her. She's just a few hours away."

Seconds jump by in silence; my Cheyenne plugs onward, humming across the asphalt. The spill conquered a good four-inch swath of my right hip and since denim takes forever to dry I curse under my breath. I sneak a peripheral peek at my son, unable to detect much of anything. I hate it when he gets this quiet.

More silence. Was the ice really an accident? I return to the taillights, attempting to bury my concentration in them but not having much success. This is definitely it. This *is* the last time.

***

8:20 p.m. New York City. We hit the Queensborough Bridge at the peak of weekend traffic, the usual thicket of cars clogging the expanse, trying to squeeze their way into Manhattan. But here's the stupid part. The city of New York has apparently decided to paint the bridge during weekends, and so the traffic is down to one lane. There's orange cones all around, men in fluorescent vests running back and forth. Nick and I look up at a colossal network of giant tarps hanging throughout the assembly of rafters and beams. Since our windows are down, the light scent of latex paint sneaks its way into the truck.

"Mama, it looks like a bunch of ghosts are up there!" He laughs, his eyes fixed on the tarpaulins. It looks as if the workers are currently painting only the last half of the bridge, so the one-lane deal is only for a few hundred yards. But it still slows everything down, and it's enough to make me want to slap the mayor and the city council, the whole lot of them.

Nick sums up my frustration nicely. He bellows out, "You guys sure picked a good time to work on this bridge!" Exactly. But wait, who the hell's he talking to?

I look over and see that it's one of the painters, clad in a green-splotched jumpsuit, gloves and hat; he's just a few yards away, out by the bridge railing, and he's squatting, fiddling with the end of a tarp that's dangling down, apparently come loose. Nick is able to talk to anybody—a gift I never had—and the painter appears to be the same way.

"Excuse me?" He looks at us, a big, cheeky smile, and as Nick repeats what he's said, the painter begins to nod, cuts him off.

"True, true. But it's *never* a good time to paint a bridge in New York. We were doing the graveyard shift but apparently that cost the city more money. So . . ."

"You work in the graveyard?"

We've now come to a stop so our new friend is right there, very present; but the compressors and sprayers are sounding off left and right, meshing right in with the backdrop of the bridge traffic, making it difficult to hear. I attempt to explain the graveyard comment to Nick, but the painter is already on it, quickly breaking down the term every which way possible. I wish he'd shut up. But he's just getting started.

"You two going to see a Broadway show or something?"

"No, we're driving out to Hainseville," Nick tells him.

"Huh?" He stops fooling with the tarpaulin and looks squarely at us.

"Hainseville."

"In Jersey?"

"Yep."

"Get out! I once painted a carport in Hainseville. Long time ago. That place is in the middle of nowhere! What takes you guys out there?"

I try to squeeze a word in but Nick is on a roll. "I'm not sure, really." He leans his head back and turns his eyes to me, as confident and as challenging as ever. "Mom . . ?"

I see the tones of Nick's father right across the bridge of his nose, along with his slanted brown eyes; just past him there's the bright green flecked all over the painter's coveralls, then the murky stretch of the East River running all the way to somewhere scary and unknown. But what's really scary is my son's despicable, knowing arrogance.

We suddenly inch forward, the crawl of the one-lane picking up. "We have some family there," I call out. "You know."

"Oh, okay," he yells, our truck rolling away. "You two have a good time!" I watch him in the mirror as he goes back to his tarp and, hopefully, the carpal tunnels that I hear many painters eventually acquire.

"He was cool!" says Nick. "Heck, maybe I'll be a painter some day."

"Nick, what did you mean back there? You weren't sure?"

"What?"

"You told that guy that you weren't sure why we were going to Jersey. You know damn well why we're going."

"Language, mom."

I hate it when he does that, even though he's right. The pace of the lane quickens and I mash the accelerator, eager to gain some ground.

"It just seems a little weird," he says. "Like, I'm not even sure who this Ruthie is."

"I told you who she was," I retort, framing a quick visual of her, or at least the way she looked the last time I saw her, some ten or twelve years ago. "She's my second cousin, and we used to be pretty close. Long ago, when we lived in Hoboken."

"I just don't ever remember meeting her."

"That's because you were barely two years old when you did! I keep telling you that!"

My eyes go from his back to the windshield, just in time to see the brilliant red of brake lights, mere yards away. I pound the brakes and we screech to a stop, just avoiding the rear end of a black Volvo. Nick's body lurches forward and he throws his hands up, slamming against the dashboard.

"Mom! Come on!"

"*You're* the one that's arguing about where we're going!" I catch my breath and notice two new painters out near the railing, mixing something in a five-gallon bucket. One of them looks up at us, no doubt noticing how loud we are.

"All I said was that it's kind of strange to be driving out to see some relative I don't know. I mean, we just finished going to see Blanchie or Blanche or whoever she was."

"Her name's Blanche. Show some respect."

"And now we're going way out to Jersey??" He sits back in the seat, straps on his seatbelt. "It just seems weird. That's all."

"There's nothing weird about it."

"To me there is. And by the way, what was up with that lady next door? Out there cramming the back of her car with all that baseball junk. She didn't steal that stuff, did she?"

"No. Of course not."

"Well. This whole trip just seems a little strange."

"We are done talking about it," I say, smacking my palm against the fat part of the steering wheel. "For the final time, this might be the last chance I get to see my cousin. Now, let it go."

The traffic picks up again and I steal another sideway glance at Nick. But its official: this time he's looking right at me. My focus returns to the taillights of the Volvo, to the waning stretch of the bridge, but my mind is back to a familiar area. I'm wondering just who in hell wears the pants in the maturity department, me or my nine-year-old. It's not the first time I've pondered such a ludicrous question.

One such time happened a couple of years ago, during a chaotic dining experience at Jay's Diner. There must have been one-hundred Boy Scouts in that restaurant, running around, excited from a field trip they'd just returned from. Our drinks took forever, our food took even longer, and the check, well, the check never came; so after repeated attempts at flagging down our frenzied waiter I grabbed Nick's hand and we waltzed out of there. *We tried to pay*, I assured him as we drove off in a flurry. *Right?* But he just stared at me, kept staring at me as I drove. I turned on the radio, tried to make small talk; but there was something deafening about the look he gave me.

Another time was after a late-night girls-night-out in my living room. After a long week at work, me and some friends had let loose a little steam, and I woke up the next morning, stumbling into the kitchen for my Folgers, my senses slapped by the sounds of Yosemite Sam and his six-gun. Empty bottles of wine sat out, an ashtray teeming with cigarette butts, beer bottles stationed on every table. Nick sat on the carpet, fixed on the the tube.

"Sure is a big mess in here," he said, his eyes never leaving the television screen. The cartoon raged on as I made my coffee and looked out the kitchen window, silent, angry at having been in no shape to clean everything up. *Did I even know my own son?* This little boy, who often reminded me of the watchful, preachy neighbor, taking in everything from his rocker across the street?

***

9:10 p.m. Somewhere in New Jersey. We're parked on the side of the road, amidst the weeds and brush, the fat clumps of sassafras bumping against the truck's fender. I study the rear-view, watching the uniformed jerk make his way to us from his car. Jersey's finest has got us and they've got us good.

"How fast were you going, mama?" asks Nick again, turning to look through the back window.

"Not sure," I say, knowing good and well that we were well over seventy-five. He's now right at my window, the patrolman, with his big hat and flashlight. I pass him my license and we go through the whole routine. He walks back to his car with my ID to check everything out, and I'm trying to calculate the hit a potential ticket will make in my little shoe fortune. Then there's a random memory and I've got the jitters. *Did I pay that parking ticket that I got in Albany?* But no. That was in New York, not Jersey, and I knew the patrolman's computer wouldn't pick it up.

"Mama, why are you smiling? Aren't you about to get a ticket?"

I turn to my son, fed up with his subtle sarcasm. "Excuse me?"

"He's gonna give you a ticket, right?"

But Johnny Law is already back at my window, the fresh ticket in his hand. He's looking at the back of the truck.

"Looks like your tarp is coming loose," he says, directing his light across the bed.

"Um, my what?"

"This tarp you have back here," he says. "Part of it was flapping in the wind when I pulled you over. Want me to secure it for you?"

I shake my head swiftly.

"Let him do it for you, mama," Nick pipes up. "You don't want it to fly away, do you?"

I'm not able to formulate the venomous words that I want to use on Nick. But he's not finished. "It's not a big deal. It's just an old tarp, mom. Right?"

I look at the officer, speechless, locked with indecision, but he seems to read me just right. "Suit yourself, lady," he says, shoving the ticket at me. "All the information is right here. Make sure you read the fine blue print, at the bottom." He adjusts his hat, shoots another look at the bed of the truck. "Try and slow it down some. This is not the I-95, you know."

I grunt a thank-you as he walks off, then fire up the engine. But Nick has his door halfway open. "Let me take care of the tarp. I'll be quick."

"No," I lay it down, anxious to get on the road. He's got his leg halfway out the door, but I've got the Cheyenne in drive, the truck rolling forward.

"Mom!"

"We are leaving, son. Now leave that tarp the way it is."

"It won't take but a second!"

I say nothing, letting the acceleration of the truck speak for me. He slams the door and we roll out of the sassafras and weeds, back onto the asphalt. A Bonnie Rait tune seeps quietly from the radio, and as Nick mutters something under his breath, we approach fifty, now sixty, sixty-five. After about ten minutes he puts his head against the door and closes his eyes. That's right, mister Nick. *Shut your eyes.* I've had enough of you for one day. Go to sleep so I can take care of business. Another hour or so and we'll be there.

***

10:27 p.m. Hainesville, New Jersey. Arthur's Attic doesn't look like it's changed much. A one-story cinder-block building, paint peeling. Hideous. A parking lot riddled with potholes and dried mud. There's but one exterior light, a tiny fixture dangling from a telephone pole off to the far left, and to the right of the building a narrow path cuts through a strip of weeds and briars, leading to a side door. I shut the engine off and sit there, staring at the ugly facade, moved by the temptation to high-tail it back to aunt Blanche's and fling the cleats out onto her neighbor's lawn.

But, no. Nick's heavy breathing brings me back. I look down at him, lying on his side, snoring away, and then I quietly step out of the truck.

I'm such an idiot that I didn't even think to bring something for protection, just in case. A crowbar, or a stick, perhaps? The Hindenburg transaction was quick and smooth, but that was three years ago and maybe the old man now has something different in mind. I walk numbly around the corner of the building and instantly it's not dark but *black*, cave-like; I reach for the buzzer, a million of those television murder dramas zooming through me. But Frank is now right there, in the doorway. He flashes a set of stained teeth and I hear myself stuttering. "Uh, um, hello?" It's one of those moments where the fear is so thick that it leaves you stupid and mule-like, your brain scrambling to brace itself for anything.

"Well?" he says, his voice much more high-pitched than I remember. "Where are the shoes?"

I cough a few times, then barely manage to squeak out, "This way."

The shoes, yes. I'm no history freak, nor a baseball fan. Just a struggling mom who's sick of not being able to provide. But the Hindenburg, I eventually learned, went down in a staggering forty-five seconds, and one of its passengers, a cabin boy named Weiner Herz, actually leaped to the ground from the gargantuan fireball as it descended, virtually scratch-free. So I know that I'll soon enough sit down and read all about Mr. Ty Cobb and his many feats on the baseball diamond. The doubles that he hit, the bases that he stole, all while wearing the baseball cleats that are the whole reason for this road trip. But right now my only concern is the deafening blackness that blankets this little corner of Jersey. How the fact that nothing is said as we walk to

my truck—me first, Frank behind me—is nearly suffo-
cating me. Say something, for God's sake.

At the truck, I break the silence. "Here we go," I
offer, lightly tapping the dented side of my Cheyenne,
pointing to the bed. A surge of confidence hits me, ripping through my shoulders, down my right arm as I
reach over and yank off the tarp. *You better have the
dough, Pops.* I'm done. I'll get this money and we'll
have a little abundance, for once. And then no more. I
hate feeling like a lowlife crook. Because that's something that I'm not.

What I am, though, is tongue-locked and mute, my
senses waylaid. Because there is no box. No Cooperstown stamp. No Cobb's cleats.

I skip through the impossible scenarios, the brain-
bending possibilities. The stops that Nick and I made.
McDonalds. Powdered donuts and juice at the Tom
Thumb. A bathroom break at some run-down barbecue
joint. Where else . . .?

"Lady," mutters Frank. "What gives? What are you
trying to pull?"

Was the box in the back when the cop pulled us
over? At the gas station, when Nick ran inside for beef
jerky? Did I see it?

What I do see is my son staring at both of us. He's
got the door open, craning his head out, rubbing his

sleepy eyes. Looking like the sweet nine-year-old boy I sometimes forget he can be.

"Mama, where are we? What are you doing?" He looks at Frank, then quickly back at me. The light casts a thin pallor across the creased face of Frank, who's giving me that *start talking* look. It's pretty obvious this isn't his first rodeo.

"The boy asked you a question," he says. "Aren't you going to answer him?"

Is this the kind of thing Nick and I will both laugh at when I'm dropping him off for college orientation? When we're eating cake at his wedding, sitting amidst balloons and white lattice, live jazz filling the air?

Or is this something that's going to make him ashamed of being my son?

Or me, of being his mother?

I stare at both of them weakly. I know that I'll soon find out.

☞ 5

A Degree in Sociology

When you don't press too hard, the wheel of the grinder works on its own, lightly ripping through the window frame's ancient layers of putty and paint, shooting the latex particles out into the summer air. The windows were in horrendous shape, which is why you put them off until last. *Zzzzmmt. Zzzzmmt.* The wheel flattens against the wood and you guide its rotations, watching the tiny chips spray left and right. Dennis is always barking reminders to put on a respirator but the mask makes you hot and uncomfortable, and at thirty-six, you often give up on safety and instead opt for comfort. Especially in an occupation that is routinely uncomfortable. And especially on this underbid job.

You turn off the grinder and cast a look down at the corner of the house where Dennis is working. "Don't worry," he says. "You're all right." He pulls his Wooster brush out of the shiny bucket and works the glossy paint, pepper can red, across the thick blades of one of the home's shutters. You nod, appreciative of his awareness. Paint dust let loose by the fury of a grinder can give others working nearby a conniption. You've seen it, you've done it, and since the job is paying diddly it's the absolute last thing you want.

It's Friday, just before noon, the tenth day on the job. And though everybody always thinks that the weather here in the southern chunk of California is Tahiti-like, when you're working a grinder in the middle of August and the sun is in full force there's a different perspective. Your bra is coated with sweat, your dirty-blonde hair is chock full of paint chips and dust, and you hate the way your panties constantly need reworking because of all of the stooping, bending and climbing associated with the work.

"When was the last time," your aunt Jackie once suggested at a family get-together, "a woman on a hot job site could pull off her shirt? The way that men do?"

Your father, sitting across the room, picking at a bowl of Jello, just snorted dismissively. It's bad enough that you generally avoid working near the high-traffic areas of some job sites because of the constant catcalls and stares. *Is that really a girl doing this kind of work?* But whatever. You and aunt Jackie have had plenty of discussions about women in construction, of the imbalance of the two sexes on the job site. You're over all of that.

The grinder zips past the last corner of the window frame, stripping off the flaking paint down to the fresh gleam of the exposed oak. After running a fist across your dusty nose you begin to climb down from the ladder. But first you turn to sneak a gander at the house behind you, at the bedroom window which looms tall over the wooden fence.

When Dennis first made the discovery a few days earlier, he estimated there were hundreds of Wacky Package stickers in the room. Though the two homes are separated by the fence, once atop the six-foot ladder there's a clear visual of the entire side of the other house. Yellow clapboard siding, peeling, chipped and rotting. Monkey grass, dandelions, stinkweed knee-high, choking the sides of the foundation. But the high-light of the ladder view was a wonderful glimpse into a bedroom that contained something that has capti-vated you ever since childhood.

"Jodi, you're not going to believe what I'm looking at right now," he said. Tall and thick, Dennis looked comical straddling the top of the ladder, bucket and brush on his lap. The two of you were deep in fascia board battle, intent on being the first to finish your al-lotted section of the board that ran around the whole house; it was one of those unspoken little contests that painters have, this one especially fitting since there was an argument that morning over whose fault the under-bid job was.

The discovery helped bring some levity to the workday. "Sure that they're Wackies?" you asked him. "How can you tell?" While Dennis remained perched on the top, you climbed up to the ladder's fourth rung, peering over the fence at the window. "All I see is a bunch of junk."

Like many homes in Long Beach's Belmont Shore, the two houses are very close to each other, maybe six or seven yards apart. And with no curtains or blinds covering the window the room lay naked, warmed by the midday August heat.

"Read the sides of those boxes, genius."

He pointed to a large nightstand stacked high with green and white boxes, the telltale colors and logo on each side. The tops and sides of the colorful cardboard were stuffed and overflowing with the bright foil wrappers of packaged stickers. There were at least ten boxes, and dozens of individual packages scattered across the nightstand below.

"From this far, you can't tell exactly," he said. "But it sure as hell looks like Wacky Packages."

The rest of the room appeared dusty and unkempt, crammed with five-gallon buckets, crates of what looked to be large bags of candy, laundry baskets, an ironing board, a miscellaneous collection of domestic crap. A large bed was covered with a mishmash of newspapers, towels, and stacks of velvet and lace. But it was the vivid colors of the stickers that caught your eye.

"I know you'd love to get your paws on that stash," Dennis said, laughing as you walked back to resume the brush battle. "But seriously. Can you believe that?"

Your own sticker collection is not large. If you're not affixing them to random items around the apartment, you usually give them to your two little nephews, pieces of flat bubble gum stashed in-between the stickers, which just ticks off their mother. Since childhood, you've bought the goofy decals in spurts, a few packages here, a few there, on through middle school, sometimes even in high school. In recent years you've returned to your fixation of the colorful collectables, purchasing them online, in convenience stores, usually when you are alone. "How old are you?" your sister once asked, as she stared at the row of spoof stickers on your refrigerator door. *Cheepios. Kiss Kat. I Can't Believe It's Not Better!* Old enough, you thought, to understand that putting an age limit on a hobby was stupid. The vibrant colors and the satiric simplicity of Wacky Packages have always left you enamored, and that's something you don't think should cease just because of age. What was so hard to accept about that?

You tap the grinder lightly on your knee and continue to stare at the room, squinting hard at the piles of junk. Dennis's taunting voice rings out from the corner of the house. "Don't stare too hard." He runs his brush across the top edge of the shutter, his smirk as consistent as the California sun. "Or when we finally leave this job you'll regret not going for it."

Your cousin is always the daring, mischievous type, something you sometimes appreciate since the monotony of the day can be excruciating. Sneaking a handful of oatmeal cookies from an unattended kitchen plate at that job in Torrance. Rearranging the family photographs on the mantle at a customer's house in Anaheim, an uptight woman whose nerdish ways were just unbearable.

But breaking and entering? Is that what this would amount to? Would aunt Jackie smile at such an idea?

"Just looking," you lie. "I thought I saw somebody in there."

"Nobody's in that house. I've been keeping an eye on the driveway." Dennis wears his hair crew-cut style, and the sun has baked his cantaloupe-shaped head evenly, on all sides. As he talks, he holds his brush in the air like a portraitist studying his canvas. The high noon heat strikes the glistening bristles, and the bright sheen of the red paint is so searing that you have to turn the other way.

"If somebody were in there," he goes on, "we would have heard them park and get out. That house is abandoned. But relax. I won't tell mom you were scared."

"What? *Scared?*"

He grins and turns back to his brush. "You heard me."

Though he's your business partner and does bring a level of animation to the workday, Dennis's loud and prankish ways are nothing like his hip but reserved mother, one of the few glimmers of reason in your life. Unlike literally everybody else, aunt Jackie generally knows what to say and when to say it. *Scared* is the last thing she would call anybody. You brush the dust from your lightly freckled arms, reasoning like you often do that aunt Jackie is part of why you've partnered with Dennis for so long. The way she dispenses advice over iced tea and snacks. The way she used to sit in her giant orange beanbag, knitting while you played her garage sale bongos, those many after-school afternoons spent at your aunt's house.

She can often be found in her cluttered kitchen—the glint of her nose ring ever-present—rustling up a quick workday lunch for you and Dennis, listening while you complain about the latest round of drama from your father. Listening. One of her many strong points.

"Your dad is angry, Jodi. Always has been. No use getting worked up over *his* getting worked up. He's the one that has to get up in the morning and choose his attitude." It was the way she said such things.

"Let him live, you know? Hell, that goes for all men. Let 'em live." She handed you a paper plate of egg salad sandwiches, neatly sliced in halves. "No use in trying to change a few millennia of ingrained habits."

***

Aunt Jackie's egg salad sandwiches. It's lunchtime and you'd give your left breast for one of those delicacies right now. Loxpoli's might advertise the *best roast beef in southern California!* but on this particular day it's doubtful. You ball up what's left of the dry sandwich and stuff it in the bag while Dennis happily chomps away. When hungry, Dennis could eat the insides of a deceased goat. As he works the sandwich he drips grease and mayonnaise across the front of his paint-splotched wife-beater, down onto the hair of his thick, sunburnt arms.

"I've been thinking," he says in between massive bites. "I figure if we finish this job by Monday we'll be okay."

"It's still a loss, overall."

"I know it. We both know it. But by Tuesday we'll be done with Tim, and on to the next job. Who do we have next, that customer in Garden Grove?"

You nod but continue to fret over the sequence of communication that brought about the underbid job. The initial conversations with Tim—a teacher at a local university who Dennis has officially dubbed 'the professor'—were easy and relaxed, but something somewhere went wrong. *You told him three thousand? I thought we agree on four.* No, that was for the house and the garage! *You didn't specify that!* But we talked about it!

Such mixed-up communication rarely happens but there are occasions when things go loosey-goosey with a customer, leading to a verbal contract from only one of you, and before you know it, things have gone south. With the professor, this was one of those times.

"Well," Dennis continues, wiping a glob of cheese from his chin with his pinkie. "Let me do the talking with this next customer so we can avoid confusion. He's that big Mexican guy I told you about. He's an old-timer. A former wrestler. In his living room there's all these pictures of him in those stupid wrestling masks they used to wear."

"Really?"

"Yep. Sucker must weigh three bills. Let me talk to him. I think he's a real machisto tough-guy type."

The frustration from the underbid job now slides into a new realm: so *what* if he's a machisto Latino? You can—and usually do—talk to the customers more effectively than Dennis. Why do men seem to be the immediate go-to when the need for a good communicator arises?

While Dennis busies himself with his phone, you pull out a bag of Reese's Pieces, your secret stash, and head back to work. No need to share since the roast beef wasn't satisfactory. On the side yard, the ground is riddled with paint rags, roller frames, dozens of tubes of caulk, and as you search the sea of tools for your five-in-one, the window is right there, just above the fence, tempting you. Speaking to you. Someone simply died, right? Is that it? A reclusive widower, a hoarder. Someone who's now gone on to glory, whose wonderful possessions will all wind up in probate. In a dark storeroom somewhere in Long Beach.

Or maybe a family member will soon arrive and clean everything out. That's what will happen. A greedy granddaughter, trying to score a mini-profit on E-bay. You stand at the fence, staring blankly, munching on your chocolate. Just overhead, a trio of Half Moon parrots flits by, their cawcaws ringing through the palms and pines.

"I told you about that." It's Dennis, who's just walked up behind you, still smacking on his food. You can barely understand him but his challenge is barely veiled.

"No use looking at that house if you aren't going to do anything."

You hesitate before answering. "What if they're just baseball cards?"

"Jodi, wake up. You saw the colors and the logo on those boxes. They're Wackies. I mean, why do you think there's so much candy in that room?"

"I don't know."

"Whoever lives there probably used to deal all that stuff wholesale or something," he says. "They probably just died and nobody knew what to do with all of it."

The machisto Mexican wrestler skips through your mind. And then comes this underbid job, the incredibly small amount of money being made. You turn to look at Dennis. Your cousin, whose lips are still lathered with bits of roast beef and grease; your cousin, who generally means well, but whose sarcasm and taunting can climb aboard your very last nerve.

"Is the other ladder still in the backyard?" you ask.

"Leaning against the fence. Right where you left it."

"Come on, then. Let's do it."

"What?"

"You heard me," you deadpan like a dictator, pointing to the back of the house. "We're doing this, cousin."

"Is this the older and more mature Jodi that I'm actually hearing? The niece of my distinguished mother?" He runs his fat tongue around the inside of his mouth, collecting the rest of his food, and after

swallowing breaks into his usual grin. His head is all
the rounder when he smiles.

"Move it," you retort, shoving the bag of candy into
your pocket, then pushing his chest lightly with the
five-in-one. "Before I change my mind."

"Oh, don't do that, he says with a whirl, marching
towards the backyard. "I love it when you're like this.
I'm in like Flynn."

***

You're already wondering how to explain this to
aunt Jackie. Though your aunt is the hippest fifty-five-
year old around, she has still maintained a simple, fun-
damental sense of right and wrong. And she's done so
without being preachy or critical, a quality that her
brother—who doubles as your father but might as well
be your brother since he acts like one—never attained.
Evident by his loud, liberal opinions. Evident by lots
of other things. After you and Dennis easily spirit over
the fence it becomes obvious that nobody's lived at the
house for a long time. A collection of old tires, sofa
cushions, rusted-out lawnmower frames are strewn
throughout the thick grass. The fence encloses the entire yard so the break-in might be easier than expected.
You step through the thicket of weeds and assorted
junk and climb the cinder block stairs to the back
porch, one of those wraparound types with a mishmash

of long wooden slats, pocked throughout with holes and rot.

Dennis hops up on the porch and begins to lithely and dramatically step around the rotting planks, doing his Indiana Jones routine.

"Come on!" he kids. "We have to get the holy stickers."

"Quiet," you hiss.

"Quiet? Girl, nobody's even here. Relax. We're about to cash in on sticker heaven." Dennis's ape-like arms are big and present, tiny sprinkles of paint flecked all through his hair, and you wonder how his wife puts up with all that.

There are a million padlocks on the back door, along with a plethora of official-looking papers stapled all over the place. Los Angeles County Board of Supervision. Occupational Safety Association. California Inspection Code 51X. One paper in particular, a blue document, catches your eye, but then there's a light rattling sound and you turn to see Dennis already checking one of the porch windows, jimmying the bottom of it with his caulk-encrusted fingers. He shakes the window, rattling it left to right, and then slides it upward, the soft *shusshhh* music to your ears.

"You gotta be kidding me!" he says, pushing the bottom of the sill up squarely with both palms. "The temple's not even locked!" The last time he was this excited was the last day of a big apartment job square in the middle of Compton, the two of you pulling out of the driveway, exuberant and giggly at not having any troubles. He climbs through the window quickly, still doing the Indiana Jones bit.

And there it is. There is no hallway or kitchen to tiptoe through, for it's *the* bedroom, right here, right now. The room has more clutter than you thought. Cardboard bins stuffed with old letters and postcards. Record albums stacked a mile high. Newspapers everywhere. The scent of age and neglect smacks you broadly, the stink of moth balls and mustiness, all of it bringing to mind aunt Jackie's woman-cave, an unused bedroom in her house that's gradually become her own little temple of oddities and clutter.

Dennis walks right over to the room's nightstand, on a mission, but you're still absorbing everything, taking in all of the untouched antiquity. Something about such a forlorn setting has always stirred an excitement deep down, and you wonder if that's because of aunt Jackie's hoarding inclinations.

Which Dennis confirms. "This reminds me of mom. I know you could spend all day in here and take in the nostalgia. But come on. Here they are."

The boxes and the nightstand look as if they've been sprayed with dust. Dennis runs his palm across the top of one of the lids, cleaning it off, and after placing the box on the edge of the mattress and opening it, your eyes are aglow with the kaleidoscopic reflection of one of the only things that's ever brought out the child in you. There's easily one-hundred packs inside, the bright squares lined up one after another. At eight to ten stickers per pack, you look at the other boxes and quickly do the math, determining that Dennis's guesstimate was much too conservative. Beautifully conservative. Would they really take a middle-aged woman to jail for lifting someone's long-forgotten stickers?

"Well? What do you think?" Dennis asks, squinting through his sweat, grinning like a mule after a full meal. It's obvious that he's giving you the option of making the first move, deferring to his elder cousin. You meet his merry eyes, and after another sweep of the record albums, the blankets and fabric, the dark-paneled walls, this lovely snapshot of a time gone by, you pick up three boxes of stickers and whirl towards the door.

"Time to giddap, Indiana," you say. "Vámonos."

It all started with a degree in sociology. That's usually what you tell people. That what-the-hell-do-I-do-with-this-diploma misery that immediately set in after the cap and gown ceremony. There was a brief stint in management at Clyde's Apparel, which gradually worked its way around to weekend painting with Dennis, eventually becoming simply 'painting.' You're still not sure how this last leg of the journey became an everyday thing. But nine years later you haven't left, still working in an industry that contains so few females. Your hands are chapped and dry, and the milkshake-thick lotion you soak them in helps but has never brought back the tender skin from another time. And it sure as hell doesn't ease the carpal tunnels that has begun to set in.

You wince slightly as you raise the boxes to your chest, the nerves in your left hand crying out; despite the pain, childhood manages to flap through your mind, those afternoons at the Super Stop purchasing candy and Wacky Packages, hanging out at Dennis and Aunt Jackie's before finally walking home. You're slapped with an electric reality: *Yeah, baby. We are doing this!*

But something breaks, a loud *snap*, and what you're doing is looking down in horror at your left foot, crunched right through one of the old floorboards, submerged in darkness. From behind, Dennis bumps you in the back, burying your foot even deeper.

"Jodi, what the hell are you doing?"

You yank your foot upwards but the instant pain suggests you cease and desist. The floor has it trapped like a steel vice.

"Damn, Sam!" He stoops to get a closer look. "You can't pull it out?"

"I'm trying." With each tug the hardwood planks on both sides pinch your ankles tighter and tighter. Pain creeps in even heavier, and sudden visuals of the emergency room followed up by a trip to the police station swim through the tears that are now blurring your vision.

"It hurts, Dennis. It's—it's stuck." You pull one last time, which only worsens the grip of the planks. Though your painter's pants serve as some protection you now wonder about circulation. "Go. Get a hammer or something."

"Are you sure?" Dennis is much too relaxed, which is infuriating.

"Yes! It's the only way."

"What if I grab your arms and yank you out?"

"Just go!" you shriek, honing in on the paint chips embedded in his arm hair. "Believe me, it's stuck."

He continues to assess the situation calmly, then turns to the window. "I'll get the hammer and a chisel."

It's the last thing you need, this episode that a degree in sociology has apparently led to. Would this really amount to breaking and entering? In recent months you've been hoping that your college degree can perhaps lead the way back to an air-conditioned life. A transition to sales, or maybe teaching. But having an arrest record might change that. All because of a bunch of Wacky Packages.

The spilled stickers are scattered across the floor like a Wild West card game gone bad, a demon's glossy red eyes from *Vlad Trash Bags* catching your wet eyes, dead-on. Through the window, the grinder and cord hang comfortably over the top of the ladder, and it's perhaps the only time you've ever longed to hold them.

The grip of the floor feels tighter. You attempt to count each minute that ticks by, dragging your face across your sleeve, purging the tears. Dennis doesn't need to see any of that. His tough cousin, he's always saying, would make a helluva dude, something to which aunt Jackie once retorted *why can't she just be a helluva woman?* It wasn't the first time that she called him out on his idiocy.

Dennis suddenly pops his head through the open window and produces the circular saw, along with its long extension cord, a jumbled mass in his arms. "Help has arrived, ol' girl," he says. "I'll have you out in no time!"

"You brought the saw??" The sound will no doubt reverberate through the house, out into the neighborhood. He climbs in and drags the heavy mess across the floor like a dead carcass.

"It was right at the back of the van so I just grabbed it," he says between breaths. "I couldn't find the hammer anywhere. Where the hell did you put it?"

It's too much to respond, and you just shake your head, hoping the tears are not visible. "Come on. Hurry."

The cord is still plugged in on the other side of the fence, and Dennis fights his way through the tangle in search of the end. As the prongs snap into the saw's rubber connector he looks up at you, beaming through his sweat. "Hold on tight!" It's as if you're being strapped in on a roller coaster at a carnival.

The wail of the saw has the piercing of a pterodactyl and it abruptly fills the room, the blade ripping through the ancient grains of the hardwood, evenly cutting through the plank that holds the left side of your ankle. The grip is loosened but is still tight enough to keep your foot trapped. Dennis raises the saw and steps around you to get to the other side but doesn't bother to turn the saw off, the chaotic rumble of the metal housing bumping against your thigh as he moves. "Are you out of your mind?" you yell. Dennis just gives you a quizzical stare, and you shake your head never mind, motion for him to keep on. He crouches and lowers the circular blade slowly through the wood. The thick plank remains in place but its grip is released considerably as the saw slices through it, interrupting the pressure. There are no words to describe the gushing relief as you yank your leg from the dusty hell.

"Come on," you gasp, scraping the sticker packages back into the boxes, then scooping all of it up. "Let's get the hell out of here."

Slogging through the backyard's jungle and hiking it over the fence is no cakewalk in your condition. But you manage, never so relieved to see the familiarity of a jobsite. You collapse, sprawling out on the grass, panting. Dennis, too, is a conglomerate of breath and sweat. He's on his knees, sucking wind like an out-of-shape linebacker; he then sits upright and quickly throws a drop cloth over the fallen sticker boxes, now cursing about something else.

But you've tuned everything out, throwing your head back, eyes shut, attempting to regain any sanity that a southern Californian painting contractor is supposed to have. Aunt Jackie is right there, her yellow scarf and large brown eyes roaming through the blackness of your closed eyelids. *Your dad's always been angry, hon. Just live and let live.*

Would her words eventually transcend to *she made a mistake, boys. A simple mistake?* A powwow with your two nephews on the vices and bad decisions of their once-respectable aunt?

A chipper, birdlike voice rings out. "Hello? Guys?"

It's the professor, right on time. But then there's also the continued grumbling and movement of Dennis, and when glancing over you see the reason for his agitation. The shutter paint is now a pond of red enamel, crawling out of a five-gallon bucket that has tipped over during your crash-and-burn re-entry. Dennis pushes the sticker boxes up against the side of the bucket, covering most of it with the same drop cloth. He's still cursing, which just chaotically meshes in with the repeated chorus of *Hello? Hello?*

Tim is standing right at the front corner of the house. He's dialed right in, horn-rimmed glasses, a fresh shave, professional posture, the whole shebang. He's just far enough to not see anything out of the ordinary.

"Oh, *there* you two are," he calls out. "How are you guys? Getting a little work done?" He's wearing khakis and a button-down shirt starched so tight that it looks like it would hurt to wear.

"Doing fine, Tim," answers Dennis, sitting back, doing his best to appear natural. "Just taking a little break back here." You smile weakly and wave, praying that he stays where he is.

"That's good!"

Of course it's good. *You got a one thousand dollar coupon on this paint job.* Why wouldn't it be good?

"Hey, I wanted to ask you. You two weren't over knocking on the neighbor's door, were you?"

Overhead, the darting parrots and the limbs of the palm trees have this wonderful crisscrossing pattern against the afternoon light of Long Beach. But everything—no matter how beautiful—comes to a ferocious halt, and this existence is frozen. Did he just ask what you think he did?

Dennis manages to spit out a few words. "Uh, no. Why?"

"Oh, sorry," the professor gushes, almost apologetically, which brings some relief. "Well, one of my neighbors told me last night that yesterday he saw somebody knocking on the front door."

"Oh, okay. No, that wasn't us," Dennis says. "That place is abandoned, isn't it?" He nudges your left pinkie with his work boot, lightly smirks, and it's all you can do not to slap him. *Stop gloating, idiot. We just dodged a bullet.*

"Abandoned isn't the word," Tim laughs, shoving his hands down into his crisp khakis. "The guy that lived there was an old hoarder. He has all kinds of stuff in there. He was basically evicted."

"No kidding?"

"Yep. His house and yard were both a health hazard, and some of the neighbors have complained for years. The city finally came out and they gave him a few months to clean it all up."

"What happened to him?" Dennis's efforts at lengthening the conversation are flat-out annoying but you deal with it.

"Oh, he was really old, and honestly, sort of losing it. His sister came over one day and tricked him into taking him to lunch, and instead moved the poor bastard into one of those elderly homes. Kind of sad, actually. Sweet old guy. But the house was full of mice and termites. And worst of all," the professor says with a bright, professional smile, pulling out his keys and twirling them on his finger like some vaudeville journeyman, "were the bedbugs. The house is infested with them. In every room. That was what really got him evicted."

You refuse to process what you're hearing as Tim steps toward his front door, still twirling his keys. He has a dinner date, says he has to go, but not without leaving you with one final tidbit.

"Yep. Long Beach is full of bedbugs. It's scary. I used to be in real estate, and believe me: when you see those bright blue papers stapled to someone's door, you know what you're in for."

As Tim walks away, Dennis throws his head back, clasping his hands together and cackling softly. Only a matter of seconds before he turns to you with that *we got away with it!* look. But all you can do is wince at the swelling in your ankle. Glare at the colossal pool of paint working its way through the pine needles and grass. And then tremble at the dirt and tiny kernels of sawdust caked across your forearms and neck, hoping that the itch you are feeling is *only* from said dirt and sawdust.

Your cousin yaks it up, and his predictability and irritating ways make you want to mash his round head down into the spilled paint, get his sweaty scalp all gooey with the bright latex. His own mother might even nod her approval at such a move. But that's immature and you know it. And aren't women supposed to represent maturity?

***

Paint dust cut loose by the fury of a grinder sometimes skips through your mind as you drive home from work. The paint dust is occasionally pixie dust straight from the lavender backdrop of *Space Flakes*, one of your favorite Wacky Packages. The anguish from operating the grinder is thick and consistent, extending on to the next workday as you're caulking door jambs, maybe working the heavy roller pole across a ceiling. *Does Dennis have these kinds of thoughts?* You wonder about the factory employee responsible for tediously inspecting each Wacky Package before the final phase of packaging, wonder if he too experiences such worksite anguish.

Another thought: does ice really reduce swelling? Dennis swore by it earlier, wrapping an ice-crammed Ziploc bag to your leg with tape, claiming how it saved him during high school football. As he sits behind the wheel babbling on and on about the day, you gaze out at the California sky and feel the chill seep into your ankle. Dusk has sounded its final toll, releasing long mauve-soaked shards across the I-405 horizon. Dennis steers the work van through the thicket of traffic, recounting with an idiot's glee the look on your face when you first fell into the floor.

There will be—for now—one more job, to be followed by another, the grunt of the workday, the grind of repetition, the delay of that air-conditioned life. The latex will flow, the caulk will harden, and you will soak your palms in a dish of lotion every night after work. And Dennis will be Dennis.

But today there was a victory, an absolute celebration of your gender. Enough with the Huck Finns of the world, the rabble-rousers and adventurers that are praised and fawned over. If boys will be boys, then *women can be women*. Right, aunt Jackie? There is no shame in today's breaking and entering, at this new venture that can gradually become the norm, you tell yourself. The waning stretches of light color the tops of the boxes of Wackies lying in your lap. The tiny fang-like scratches on your forearms bite slightly, wounds, you've determined, merely acquired during the quick getaway. You'll take your punishment like a *woman*. An attitude that will perhaps one day stick in the vernacular of our times.

You grit your teeth and push this new reality through your tired vision, out through the latex-flecked windshield. Dennis howls on and on, like a confused baboon. You are thrilled with today's catch, hoping that it contains *Ant Jemima* or *Cream of Feet,* those long lost Wackies. But you are especially hopeful that aunt Jackie will relish in what you've done, this new reality that you've attempted to carve out. This deed that began with a degree in sociology.

☞6

Friday the 13th and Folgers

Y ou stand in the kitchen doorway, clicking
your nails against the receiver to the ugly
marmalade-orange telephone while tak-
ing in the whole of Uncle Earl. He's sprawled out in
the ancient recliner. His massive frame heaves up and
down, working in time with his noisy snoring. *A freight
train run loose of the tracks couldn't wake me*, he once
said over corned beef hash and iced tea, back in those
first few days when you and Joey were staying with
Earl, just getting to know him. You held Joey's hand

and laughed it up, looking at the rural emptiness all around.

But now you stare at the telephone and fight off the sickening idea of ripping the long curly cord from the receiver and wrapping it around Earl's fleshy neck, putting an end to this madness, this ridiculous way of living.

It's still several hours before your double down at the Stagecoach Diner. You softly close the screen door, step out onto the dusty pine slats of the wraparound porch. This is one of the few times of the day to think and be alone. You and a warm cup of Folgers, out here in the early fog, staring at the swampy backyard, the steam slipping up from the thick woods of lower Alabama. *Shame, shame* for having those vicious thoughts about the telephone cord.

They rolled the fog machine in during the second week of shooting. And though the movie was lame it still gave you the willies as you did your little six-minute scene; after Jason slit your throat, the thick red corn syrup gushed like an open spigot, and you collapsed, dead. But then you squinted out at the fog, wondering just how it was all going to appear on the big screen. You also pondered if the role would lead to more roles—bigger and better films that featured young, black actresses. You weren't so sure. The mist crept slowly, enveloping the feet of the film crew and production staff, seeping out into the air just above the clay banks of the large pond, which in the film was dubbed Crystal Lake.

But like the laughter and good times with Joey, all of that was during an earlier time, when things were new, even adventurous. That was the state of *before.* For you, the mood in Stockton, Alabama is now different.

"Sidney?" Uncle Earl calls out from inside, waking up.

"Yeah?"

"Can ya help me into my chair, please? Looks like it's gonna be one of those days."

One of those days usually means more work. There are occasions in which he can get around with his cane or wheelchair, not needing much help. But lately you're convinced that those days are outnumbered by the others. Earl holds your elbow and pulls his body up with one arm while gripping the arm of the wheelchair nearby with the other, readying his large frame for the transition. You brace your legs and lower body, used to this, even though it always leaves a slight tweak in your lower back.

"Honey, you enjoyin' the morning air back there?"

"Yes, Uncle Earl." *Was* enjoying the morning air. "It's nice." You exhale rapidly as he drops into the seat of the wheelchair, releasing your arm at the last second, bringing instant relief.

"Wonder where all this fog's been comin' from," he says, his chest now panting slower as he situates his frame comfortably in the seat. He begins to roll back to his bedroom. "Leaves everything damp and wet."

You stretch your back out and suck in a few breaths of your own as he rolls down the hall. Just over his shoulder hangs a hockey mask on the wall, a hip souvenir you lifted from a prop box on the set when nobody was around. Jason Voorhees was the only real star of *Friday the 13th VII*, but even he was just a guy in a jumpsuit and a mask. Not necessarily William Hurt or Jeff Daniels that you were sharing credits with. It was a gig all the same, three days of shooting that put nine-hundred dollars in your pocket, the first film credit under your belt.

But then the catastrophes started. Earl took a hard fall on the front porch, dislocating his hip. Joey bolted for the lure and magic of Hollywood. And before you could blink you were stuck in Stockton. Stuck with this man, this Uncle Earl, who in some respects was exactly like your grandfather. A reclusive, old bachelor that had very few people in his life.

Out on the back porch again, you hold your coffee and enjoy the spook of the air, letting your eyes penetrate the thick mist. You simply don't have the heart to leave him. Though at first there was some kind of satisfaction at the free room and board and the chance to spend a little time down in the sticks of southern Alabama, things are now different. 1. Shooting for the film is over, production has wrapped up, left town. 2. Joey is *no mas.* 3. Earl is, well, he's lumbersome. Cumbrous. No, he's *colossal.* The tiresome television babble of Bob Barker comes shooting out of Earl's bedroom, the same morning noise you've put up with for the last five weeks. And as the bright orange telephone cord jumps through your mind for a quick encore, you ask yourself once again: can you really do this until Christmas?

***

Tips were good that evening. Sally, another waitress, wipes down one of the large oak tables with a wet towel and then turns to you with a wide grin. "Figured I made sixty or seventy bucks tonight! Not bad, huh?"

"Yeah, I made close to that, I think," you say, refilling the bottles of ketchup and mustard. It's just past nine, and the last customer, a tall, scarecrow-like man wearing greasy overalls, is sitting in the back corner, swallowing down the last of his cornbread and okra.

"Did you call that guy back about the play? He was in here again yesterday. He keeps askin' about you, Sid. You know you're now famous around here."

And he can keep asking. You have no desire to perform the role of Cleo in *Rocket to the Moon* at the Tiny Tim Theater.

"I've got his number written down somewhere. I'll call him. Uncle Earl always has the TV on real loud in the house so it's hard to be on the phone with anybody."

The tube *is* always on in the house, and the noisy commercials and silly sitcoms are just unending. "My hip doesn't bother me as much when I kin watch my stories and my game shows," Earl once said with that big, goofy laugh, his broad chest jiggling as he slapped the dusty denim that stretched across his wide thighs.

You count your money while walking through the kitchen past the ice machine and dishwasher. The dishes are stacked up eight or nine plates high, nudged in beside pitchers of melting ice. Clumps of spilled collards and peach cobbler are slopped all over the chrome counter. You run the one-dollar bills through your fingers. Twenty, now thirty, here a five, there a five. Tips have been consistent since you began working at the diner, and after tucking the money away, your swelling bank account comes to mind. Without apartment rent or a regular grocery bill, it's suddenly been easy to put away some dough. But then you bristle with anger at these thoughts of sudden contentment.

Sally comes bustling through the back, shouldering a platter of silverware, dishes, baskets of bread, and half-full pitchers of tea. "Come on," she beckons, "I want to hear you sing." She lets out an A-flat, and doesn't sound half-bad for a country girl with no training past high school.

"Sally, why aren't you active in theater?" you ask, taking the platter from her hands. "Is your husband that busy with the archery team?"

"You mean, the *Stockton* Archery Team," she corrects you. "Girl, that's all he does." She wipes her hands on her white apron and starts placing everything onto the counter. "He claims that since he's paying most of the bills he should have first dibs on any free time."

Andre, a sixty-something man with a gentle demeanor, takes some of the dishes and scuttles them hurriedly into the washing area. He's soft-spoken, with a pair of bright grey eyes that twinkle when he talks.

"But damn," you say, astonished, "you work too."

"He says that part-time doesn't count. I can follow my fairytale when Whitney starts kindergarten." She looks at you with that oh-well shrug.

You shake your head and suddenly hate everything about lower Alabama. A stack of plates falls over hard, splashing water and coffee grinds everywhere. You jump back, barely able to escape the dark, grainy spray. *Does everybody in this godforsaken wasteland drink Folgers?*

"No word from Joey?" Sally asks, looking as thoughtful as you've ever seen anybody. Though you are generally disgusted with where you are living, you determine that people in the country can really be pleasant and downright genuine. Even to a black girl.

"Nope. Nothing."

"Girl, how long's it been? Three weeks?"

"Yeah. I guess so," you say, studying a tattered poster hanging high over the time clock, a dusty advertisement for an old production of *Peter Pan.* "Something like that."

It's been a month since Joey took a bus down to Mobile, from where he caught a flight to southern California. Joey's cousin is a writer for *LA Law*, and had promised him something if he were to make the big move out West. "Sidney, it may only be some kind of internship or a go-get-me-my-coffee deal," he told you. "But it's *something*. I'll keep you posted."

Andre bangs two more plates against the garbage can, tosses the dishes into the sink. The tiny Folgers grinds and the soggy crust of neglected peach cobbler swim towards the drain. And as you watch Sally walk back through the swinging doors you can't help but think that a go-get-me-my-coffee role might obliterate what you are now doing.

***

"Got nothing but junk mail today, honey," Earl says after you walk through the front door. "Coupons from here to Timbuktu."

He leans over a TV dinner tray, slurping the macaroni and cheese down as if he's just run a marathon. The opening bars to *Perfect Strangers* ring out from the television across the room, loud, always too loud.

"Did Joey call?" you ask, throwing your waitress apron across the back of one of the old vinyl kitchen chairs, staring at the dinner he's left out, another one of Patty's Gourmets. Because of Earl's hip, the good folks at Stockton Senior Services have provided him with a regular delivery of the meals, and right now it looks warm and downright tasty.

Earl doesn't look up from his sitcom, just shakes his head no, and commences to concentrate on his portion of fish. The tiny curls above his ears have blossomed into white with age, white as whipped cream, and you once told him how much he looked like the character Skillet from *Sanford and Son*.

The TV dinners are easy, he says, since he doesn't have to be on his feet for very long. You'd never heard of Patty's Gourmets, but it's something you've become well-versed in. Pasta and chicken, meat loaf, carrots and mashed potatoes, meatballs, linguini, and surprisingly, even steak. You grab a fork, scoop up the tray of food, and then notice a thick, buttery slab of pound cake warming in the oven. One of your favorites, and probably the third time in the last week he's tossed a pie or some such delicacy in the oven prior to your arriving home.

It's something that makes it all bearable. You're a horrible cook, never really learned, never wanted to learn. Which might explain the curvy, caramel figure that you've always maintained. Though the air is predictably warm and sultry, you sit out on the back porch, spooning bite after delectable bite of cake into your mouth while listening to the fleeting hoot of a swamp owl, darting across the pond somewhere. The moonlight is solid and ubiquitous. You stretch your legs and relax, soaking up the pond's silver backdrop while working up a quick visual of you and Joey canoeing through the dark waters. The setting is tender, the mood nice.

Until a pack of alligators rises up, yanks him in with their ferocious jaws, ravenous, now good and bloody as they chew and chomp. You watch as you casually glance down at the carnal scene, yawn, then reach over and toss his hat to the churning maroon bubbles, dessert for the gators. A single sliver of pound cake sits alone on the plate and you lean over and devour it, licking the plate and fork before looking back up and maintaining one last visual of the horrific little scene.

If only you could simply watch yourself help Earl into the shower. But now you really are dreaming. It's time for him to bathe, and though your arms are still taut from the many hours of yoga with Joey, helping Earl out in this twice-a-week endeavor is laborious. The main obstacle to the shower is the bathtub wall, which is a good two feet high. He leans on your shoulder hard and carefully steps into the stall, panting all the way.

"Ready, sweetheart? One more time." He presses down even harder on your shoulder while lifting his other leg and planting it inside the tub, the crushing weight of his body pressing a jolt of pain down into your clavicle. Uncle Earl grips the cheap hardware store handrail that you sloppily screwed to the shower wall with his Wal-Mart drill. It's hard to believe that the wobbly screws can support his gargantuan weight.

Since the only thing preventing the revolting sight of Earl's naked body is his tattered orange bathrobe you turn for the door, wondering how many more times you can perform the feat before your shoulder is snapped into pieces. It's late. You are exhausted. The ick of the diner and the grip of the humidity cling to your skin like a straightjacket. But Uncle Earl is saying something.

"Darlin?"

You turn, wondering where he's about to go with this forlorn tone to his voice.

"I know I've told you this before. But you have no idea how much that helps me, what you jes' did. Bless your little heart, darlin. I like'd to broke my neck last week when I tried gettin' in here by myself."

"Uncle Earl," you begin, regretting the overt sympathy the second the words leave your mouth. "Don't you worry about a thing. It's okay. Seriously."

"Well. I jes' wanted to tell you how much I 'preciate it."

"I know," you say, closing the door. "It's fine, really." The hockey mask peers downward as you step down the hall, and you blink hard, wincing at the sudden emotional crossfire of sympathy, revulsion, and confusion.

***

To be fair, Uncle Earl is kind, if not downright jovial. His morning serenades over coffee and waffles are at times contagious, though horrifically out of tune. He's a talker, something Grandpa Adam never was, the ten or twenty times total you spent with him before he died, years ago. *You never really got to know grandpa,* your father said after you gushed over your bit role in the movie and mentioned that it was being shot in south Alabama. "Sid, this might be the one chance to meet his only brother. Let me try and call him for you. We don't know much about him. But I hear he's a hoot!"

Earl, of course, *is* a hoot. What's more, he possesses a genuine interest in your acting and education. And though the meals are sometimes predictable, they're always warm and always on time. The pound cake doesn't hurt matters, either.

It's just difficult to believe that with his injury he's not eligible to receive anything beyond Social Security. "It's horse malarkey," he cries out one afternoon, while maneuvering through a mountain of paperwork. "The state keeps yappin' that I need my birth certificate and Social Security thingamajig but I ain't seen them in ages. They don't know the kind of sufferin' I'm in!"

"Uncle, I don't understand why you can't just get copies."

"Hon, those *were* copies. And to get copies of *those* copies you need to write to some office in Montgomery."

You make the calls yourself, poring over the blue pages of the phone book, Social Security, Medicaid, dialing the state hotline for information on elderly assistance, listening to detailed, long-winded automated messages but never actually getting around to any concrete information. You growl at the telephone, listening to the mechanized voice blaring through the orange receiver while Uncle Earl digs through a multitude of produce boxes and milk crates of papered clutter, searching. You look at the receiver and then glance back at him as he works his way through the mess, wondering if he's been honest when he says that Joey hasn't called.

"If you could jes' stay until Christmas," he says, over and over. "That's when Josie is s'posed to come down to Stockton and help me."

"Who is she?" you ask, flipping through a crinkled stack of receipts and old telephone bills.

"One of your second cousins. She lives in Atlanta."

"Oh. I think I remember her, vaguely."

"You can do that, can't ya, darlin? Till Christmas?"

The labor of sifting through the paperwork is daunting in a painful way. It could take you until Christmas to find the documents he needs. And just exactly who was this Josie?

One morning you remind him again that if Joey ever calls while you're at work to have him call the diner. Earl, though, halfway through an enormous bowl of grits and a plate of bacon, just nods and is already babbling about something else.

"Darlin, Jimmy down at the filling station was jes' tellin' me about his son, Matthew. He's that director at the Tiny Tim Theater. You need to call him, hon. It really is a good theater. Everybody around here knows that."

"I know, Uncle Earl."

"It's your kind of stuff. You know, plays and all that. Ain't there something to the stage that's more challenging than doin' movies?"

"Well, yeah, actually." You pour some Wheaties into a large yellow bowl and ponder this.

"That's what I read once in *TV Guide*. Anyway, I know you are doin' movies now but at least think about it. You might even get the lead role in that production, comin' up. What is it, 'Rockets to our Moon?'"

"Yes. I think so, uncle. *Rocket to the Moon.*" Cleo, to be exact, a major role in the play, and apparently one everybody in the community thinks is yours. You check the expiration date on the carton of milk before pouring it into the bowl. Uncle has a habit of leaving old milk in the refrigerator for weeks, something you found out the hard way.

"Hell, this could be your big start! They probably ain't never had a black girl as the main character!"

His smile is big, and with his gums covered in grits, he reminds you that he'll need groceries before long, if that's not too much of a problem. You plunge a spoon down into the cereal, concentrating on the crunchy flakes. The morning sweat creeps across your forehead, and the dusty calendar on the kitchen wall coerces your attention. The tiny boxes, the units of time, the passage of time. You think about your mother back in Birmingham, about Joey out in Los Angeles. About the fact that you are still living and working in a town called Stockton. *If you could jes' hang on till Christmas, baby girl.*

Breakfast over, he eases down the hall, one hand on the wall, the other on his cane.

"Uncle, you need my help?" you ask, praying for a reply in the negative. The prayer is answered.

"No thanks, doll," he squawks over his round shoulder. "I can manage the bathroom, thank Gawd!"

His large body becomes a voluminous shadow in the hallway, and you struggle with the frustration over what makes people like your grandfather and Earl such loners.

And then you gradually begin to marvel at how quickly human beings can adapt to the most amazing, unforeseen situations. Situations such as driving down to lower Alabama for a first movie role. Situations such as life with uncle Earl. At work that night, when Sally begins to talk about yet another movie to be shot in the area, it almost doesn't even surprise you.

"I'm not sure exactly when, but that's what I read in the paper," she says. "It's supposed to be a Steven Seagal movie. Gonna be filmed in Mobile."

"Who?"

"Steven Seagal. He's that tall dude, you know, that dreamboat that does karate and kung fu and all that. He's an actor. Built real nice, and wears a dark pony-tail. Oh gurl, he's just delicious!"

As she talks, she fishes tiny packages of toothpicks from a large box and stuffs them into her apron. "And look, you know that they filmed Close Encounters down in Mobile, don't you?"

"*The* Close Encounters?"

"Yup," she says proudly. "Mama was an extra in it. If you blink, you'll miss her. But she's there!" Sally slides plates of green bean casserole, hot rolls, and french fries onto a platter and heaves it to her shoulder. "And of course you were in *Friday the 13th*. Can't wait to watch you in that when it comes out. Shoot, girl, it's

1988. Lower Alabama ain't what it used to be! We're not California, but we hold our own!"

"Sally, stop," you say, lining up four glasses of ice water on your own platter. "I wouldn't necessarily say we hold our own." From the dishwasher counter someone's half-eaten carrot cake catches your eye, and your mind leaps to the stacks of homemade carrot cakes—Stagecoach Diner's finest—in the walk-in cooler.

"Well, you know what I mean. There are movies made everywhere, right? And those movies need extras." She walks towards the swinging door, carrying the tray with the ease of an expert. "Everybody was an extra at one time, weren't they?"

You stare through the door's circular glass windows at the purple ribbon in her hair, her head bobbing up and down as she walks, on a mission; you're grinning at her kindness and contagious spirit, and then out of nowhere you walk over, grab a spoon, and scoop a bite out of the neglected carrot cake, chewing furiously before reaching back and belting out a power chord of *lots of chocolates for me to eat*, swimming in the visual of you as Eliza Doolittle on Broadway, bringing the house down, signing autographs backstage, gulping champagne while lounging away in your little room with the star on the door.

The days dance by, reminding you to go through the boxes of transplanted junk in your bedroom. To find and update your resume and head shot, stay in the contact-making game. A phone call to your old bartending job brings some assurance, though slight, that your job is still safe.

You send postcards to your closest friends, mostly actors and artsy-types you've partied and auditioned with. Every now and again you slide a handful of dimes into the Stagecoach payphone and check in with your mother, telling her everything is fine, don't worry, you've just decided to spend some extra time with Uncle Earl while figuring this whole Hollywood thing out. With Mom, you cut to the quick and hang up. Taking off with Joey was one thing. But having such a gory, ridiculous role in such a gory, ridiculous film was something she just couldn't stomach.

Joey. You sip from a steaming mug of Folgers one morning, studying a dead oak stump out in the marshy distance. Most of the last year of your life was framed around Joey. The relationship, though, became tiresome. Even as you drove down together from Birmingham for the movie shooting, you saw that he was becoming more distant, morose. He gradually dropped hints, typical for an ambitious guy who's ready to move on. *Joey.*

You hope that a freight truck mows him down on Hollywood Boulevard, embedding his skull into Gilligan's star on the Walk of Fame.

You drink some more of your coffee. Did Gilligan *have* a star on the Walk of Fame?

***

The stick of the southern humidity lessens slightly as the early gusts and chill of autumn are ushered in. A colorful matrix of Halloween costume boxes fills the windows of Al's Five & Ten, characters like Strawberry Shortcake, the Wolfman, and Hollywood's newest horror doll, Chucky. And though you still fret over the uncertainty of the near future, you bask in the comfort and ease of mind that comes from not having to pay rent or utilities every month. Your bank account swells to nearly two thousand dollars. And as you coast down Stockton's Main Street, past Hickory Baptist Church, the diner, and the Tiny Tim Theater, you marvel at the ease of the traffic, at getting to work in under ten minutes.

And Uncle Earl? Well, he was right, you decide while driving home one evening. There *was* something to be said for the stage, for the electric nervousness that you can't just stop and do it again. The stage is real time, it's life, it's *there*, which is the way Dr. Brown would sum it up during his lectures in Contemporary

Drama. You sit in the car and stare at the front of Earl's house, at the deep brown slats of the clapboard siding. It's not yet six o'clock but it's dark, the quickening of evening brought on by the transition of daylight savings over the weekend. You've decided to sneak in and scare your uncle, bring some levity into his handicapped world.

And why not? You turn the motor off, glancing over at the faces of Casper and Wendy taped to the windows of the neighbor's house. It's not Friday the 13th but something better. Halloween.

Which recently brought about the silly idea of you and your uncle getting dressed up. Earl as the bandage-laden patient, you the creepy old nurse, maneuvering him around the neighborhood in his chair, *scaring the coon piss*, as he put it, out of the trick-or-treaters.

"It's a crazy idea," he mused, "but one that I like!" Thinking of his words, you smile while softly stepping down the dim hallway, just past the glare of Jason. But now you're curious at the bouncy swing melodies of the 1940s-style music coming from the back of the house.

A fleeting moment of a war, any war, darts across your vision, through your brain. Cannon fire, buckshot, curly telephone cord, whatever. There's no way to actually believe this. Would what you're looking at warrant starting said battle right here and now? On Halloween night?

You stand in the doorway, unable to fully process the sight of Uncle Earl in his tank top and underwear, standing, dancing a healthy jig to the music. His back is to you as he swings his heavy slab of a body left to right, and your eyes follow this little jig in absolute disbelief and disgust. The charming, scratchy sounds of the woodwinds and brass swim around the room, coming from the ancient record player in the corner. You grit your teeth, burying the impulse to drop-kick Earl from behind, and instead tip-toe backwards out of the room like a jewel thief making her getaway. The last thing you see is the crisscross mesh pattern of his threadbare tank top covering his broad, chocolate shoulders, jostling side to side as he continues on with his merry but solitaire moment. Your curiosity has become an unspeakable rage.

***

Stockton's towering pines and poplars loom in the dark distance, standing guard over the broken-down shanties lathered in kudzu, a long-forgotten Ford sinking into the Alabama clay. It's the next morning, and the street is good and slick as you drive through the early rainfall.

You left the house after Earl's little number and walked around town for hours, blank-faced and numb, watching the goblins, witches and princesses scamper up and down sidewalks. Upon returning, it took all that you had to *not* don the hockey mask, tiptoe into his bedroom and give him a coronary of the highest order. You packed your bags. Slept four hours, then left, stifling the urge to turn around and rip the curly telephone cord from the wall, wrap it tightly around his fat, fleshy neck. The absolute nerve.

Good-bye to this load of horse manure. Good-bye to all of this. Good-bye, farewells, they run through the morning of your mind, the movies and musicals, *Good-Bye Girl, Good-Bye Mr. Chips, Bye Bye Birdie.* It would only be fitting to tell Sally good-bye. Her red Pinto sits in the front parking lot, and she's on the early shift, plating hot biscuits and grits, pouring up Folgers for the crack-of-dawn crowd. Your car rolls across the wet green reflected from the diner's neon, and through the big rectangular window there's Sally, throwing her head back and laughing at something, the usual pep in her step. Your car descends to a near-stop as you watch her. The Tiny Tim Theater is just ahead, on the corner, waiting.

You drive on through the wet, six a.m. silence, wondering what Whoopi Goldberg or Jennifer Beals would say about turning down the lead role in a play, no matter how small the production. The hockey mask sits on the passenger seat. You reach over and grab it, slide it over your head, adjust the straps.

You grind your foot down into the accelerator, the front tires grabbing what they can of the wet, tired asphalt, and the car slides onward, past the last of the town's outskirts. There will come a day in which you're back to chasing down that wonderful lead role. There will be a day in which your name is etched in the bright bulbs of the marquee. But for now, Jason will do. With your taut arms locked to the steering wheel and the mask clinging snugly to your face, there are other concerns. You've never been as certain that you have no destination in mind. You've never felt as livid and swindled as you do right now.

☛ 7

Houdini in Missouri

arvin lay on the sofa, letting the tired muscles in his fifty-one-year-old body soak up the comfort from the dusty cushions. The grit of the workday's wet roller pressed through his mind, spearmint green, the chosen color for Mrs. Willa Mae's wraparound porch. Though the television news rattled on, Marvin was hardly listening. It was one of KCAT's newest evening broadcasters, this kid who was probably fresh out of the 1981 graduation class from the University of Missouri. Marvin had always found them tiresome and predictable, if not boring, the television news dud, clad in shirt and tie, sputtering down the events of the day from behind some desk.

But his ears abruptly perked up when he heard the words *Harry Houdini*. And when the newbie went on to say "Sadie Adams" and "Houdini" in the same sentence, Marvin sat up and really began to listen. Had he heard right? Something about old letters just discovered that established a link between a Robertsville local and the famed magician?

He pushed the plate of half-eaten pork chops to the side, grabbed the white rotary from the end table and dialed around, looking for confirmation. It came via his second cousin, Lena, who rarely missed the evening news.

"Yep. It was in the paper this morning, too," she said. "Apparently, them letters was in the attic of Harry Houdini's nephew or niece, or somebody. Whoever it was, they was diggin' through some old boxes and they came across 'em. Least, that's what I understood of it."

"How many were there?"

"Letters? I think they said a couple dozen. A bunch of 'em. I can't hardly believe it. Mrs. Sadie, of all people. I heard that sometimes she liked to do some magic up at the Sunday school, with the kids and all. But jeepers creepers! Houdini? In Missouri??"

Lena was a talker. Marvin sat back and studied the splotches of dried green across his light brown fingers while his cousin changed gears, now yammering about the sudden increase in her power bill and then the chicken snake she recently killed just outside her back door. She eventually wound her way back to the topic at hand.

"It just blows my mind, Marv. What in sam hill did those two talk about?"

As Lena went on blabbering, Marvin fell back into horizontal mode on the sofa while his mind sifted through the decades. He knew that Houdini had once performed one of his wild stunts in nearby St. Louis; but that was around the turn of the century, some seventy or eighty years ago. And Sadie's magic, well, a lot of Robertsville locals knew about that. For a long time, until her passing in the late 1960s, hers had been a regular stop on Marvin's handyman route. He'd maintained the shrubbery, the cedar trees, the lawn, hell, everything for the old recluse. And he'd seen the packages on the front porch, the return addresses from some magic factory in far-off Jersey. In fact, he'd seen a lot of things. He bounced the taut telephone cord across his left knee and let Lena go on and on.

After they hung up, Marvin walked out to the back porch and looked down at the roller and nap soaking in a bucket of sudsy, green water. He stretched his sore back out and peered up at the silver glow of Orion, imprinted deep in the Missouri night.

There were certainly people in the Robertsville community that had suspicions, churchgoers that exchanged whispers and rumors. *Did Sadie really know that famous escape artist Houdini?* Marvin definitely had his. One morning, after nailing her new thermometer to the porch wall, he'd turned to see her through the kitchen screen door in a pair of handcuffs. She stood there, squirming, working her wrinkled hands around the steel edges.

"Miss Sadie? Um. Need some help?"

"Oh, no. I'm just practicing.

"You sure?

"I'm sure," she said, squinting at a set of instructions on the kitchen table. "Besides, I used to have the world's best teacher."

"Who?" he asked, shoving the hammer back into his hammer loop.

She winked at him. "You wouldn't believe me if I told you."

He went to bed that night dreaming of straightjackets, of ladies being sawed in half. The next morning Marvin promptly summoned his nephew and niece, a pair of fourteen-year-old twins, from their home just down the road. He watched the two kids while sitting in his big white rocking chair and gulping his coffee. Laverne was working his way through an enormous bowl of homemade porridge, while Donna tinkered with a crossword puzzle, nibbling on a piece of bacon.

"Uncle Marvin," Laverne said, "you really think something's out there? Miss Sadie's house is nearly sunk to the ground by now, ain't it?"

"No it ain't," Donna said without looking up. "Daddy told me that Uncle Monroe went huntin' back there, in the wintertime. He said it's still there. Said it was covered in kudzu, though, and the grass was about knee-high. None of her relatives ever came to claim the house, he said."

Marvin leaned back in the rocker and ran a pair of calloused fingers across his pants. Saturday morning, an off-day. No pushing the mower or working the weed-whacker at the community center. No cleaning the windows at Magnolia Springs Baptist Church. But still a job to do. A potential paycheck to collect.

There were times in which Marvin and Sadie got his jobs and her payments mixed up; but they generally were able to work it out. All except for one particular week, in which she insisted that she'd paid him prior. They talked it out, bickered back and forth, his word against hers, and eventually it died with no real resolution. Marvin instantly began putting all future work in writing, a mini-contract for every job. But the free labor that he'd gifted Sadie gnawed at him. She was honest, he firmly believed, a decent woman. But her aging memory and their verbal contracts had gotten one over on him.

He studied the skinny frame of his niece, the attention that she gave her crossword, and then he looked at the strapping, agile shoulders of Laverne. Tough, athletic Laverne, the center fielder. But nephew had his day lined out on the ball field, and as he listened to his uncle's proposal it was clear he wasn't budging.

"I can have you back by the second game," Marvin told him.

"No can do. It's a big tournament. They said it's gonna be the biggest one of 1981! And I can't be getting there late like that. Coach said if I wanted to pitch I gotta be there all day." He ran the spoon around the top edge of the bowl, licked it clean.

"If you can't help me then why'd you walk down here?"

"You're the one that called us!" Laverne mimed Marvin on the phone. *"Got some bacon and oatmeal for you kids, come on down!"* He put the bowl in the sink, ran some water in it, and headed for the door. "You taking Donna home?"

"I can walk," she said, still not looking up from her crossword.

"Good. Thanks for breakfast, Uncle Marvin. But I need to go suit up. See ya'll."

"Want me to come with you, uncle?" piped up Donna. "I'm free all day."

He sized up his niece: light-skinned, homely, pigtails bound by red marble barrettes. Children generally got on Marvin's nerves. The only one-on-one-time he'd ever spent with the twins was when they had Saturday target practice out in the backyard. Donna had been his prize pupil, a steady hand that could pick off the Nehi bottles and Libby's cans, lined up left to right, on a fallen pear tree. It won her a few modest medals at various junior marksman tournaments around the county; but that was before makeup and boys took over. The kids were growing up, he knew, and the days in which he could really teach them *something* were more there than here.

"Yeah, I reckon," he finally said, thinking of his sister Dolores—the kids' mother—and wondered if he should talk to her first.

"You want to see if something's in there that we can give to the church carnival, right? Some old magic tricks or games?"

"Yes," he said blithely, staring out the window at the slanted ramshackle roof of his chicken coop. He then slid on his Cardinals cap, looked at the clock. *What the hell.* He was tired of riding the fence over it. There was a score to settle. A wrong to right. A lost paycheck to claim. Donna could help carry the goods to the truck, if there were any. Keep him company, if anything. Marvin knew there might be others, locals that would want to give the abandoned house a go.

"Yeah, that's right. We wanna see if there's anything we can give to the carnival. You told your momma you were comin' down here?"

"Yep."

"Okay, finish your bacon," he said, putting down his coffee mug with authority and standing up. "We need to get a move-on."

***

To call her a recluse did little justice. Sadie Adams had lived alone on a sprawling piece of property completely closed in by a barbed-wire fence, long clogged with a mess of pecan trees, azaleas, honeysuckle, and privet. To get there, you had to exit county highway 30 onto a dirt road that ran a half-mile back through the woods, which led to the three-hundred-foot stretch of clay and grass that served as the driveway. *Used to give my truck hell,* thought Marvin as he and his niece rattled along the dirt road at a steady four miles an hour. The backs of their heads bumped against the truck's rifle rack. The road was choked with grass, rocks, and colossal patches of weeds, waist-high in areas; the wire-like saplings that had shot up over time thwacked against the truck's fender and the sides of the doors.

"You gon' get a flat tire, uncle Marvin!"

"Hush. We'll be fine," he said, hoping he was right.

The house crept into view on their right, just visible through dozens of dangling dead vines. They drove a little farther, but after a few low-hanging pecan limbs slapped against the windshield he suddenly pulled over to the side of the road, just under a colossal cypress tree.

"C'mon," he said, climbing out of the cab. "The driveway's way up there, and by the way this is going, we'll never make it."

"Huh?"

"This is too much for my truck. We gon' cross the fence right here and walk out to the house."

"We gon' *what?*"

"From right here, it's not that far. Do you see it?" He walked to the side of the road, inspected the tangle of briars and bushes that crawled all over the barbed-wire. "We can climb this fence and just walk out there. Let's go. This thing is barely three feet high. Laverne could broad-jump it in his sleep."

She opened the door slowly and assessed the scene outside. "Shoot. Okay."

With a sizable share of complaining and cursing, they managed to scramble over the rusted fence. Then, they began trudging their way through a small, open field to the house. The grass was not as high as the road but just as thick, and was pocked with anthills, young maple saplings and mauve-colored cattails that had sprouted up over the years.

"I'm getting scratched up and eaten alive out here!" Donna said, bending slightly to swat at a mosquito.

"The hell did you wear shorts for?"

"You didn't tell me I was going on a safari!" she shot back.

Marvin grunted and waved his hand at her. He stepped through the brush quicker and began to focus on the house, only about fifty yards off. It was once an antebellum-style beauty, but now a rickety eyesore tucked away in time. Sheets of kudzu and dead vines coated much of the dark clapboard facade; the six-over-six windows sat cockeyed, as if the house had shifted, and many of the glass panes were cracked, some of them completely gone. He noticed that much of the lattice—though somewhat cracked and splintered—still clung to the sides of the home. A sea of briars and thick privet covered the immediate area of the house, a section of the yard that he once kept cut so tight and crisp.

The old house now loomed down over them, daunting, almost creepy. Marvin looked right up at the upper story and envisioned the thirty-foot wooden ladder he used to shinny up in order to trim the tree limbs that poked against the side of Sadie's house. *Was that the job that she didn't pay me for?* He'd performed the task every few years, and once, as he made his way down the ladder, a collection of colorful cardboard packages caught his attention, just inside an upstairs window. Illustrations dotted the sides of the packages, a cartoonish man bound in chains, a giant pair of dice. Those illustrations now made sense.

"Uncle Marvin, what are you doin?"

He was at the front corner of the house, bent over on his knees; his arm was stretched through a thicket of monkey grass and wild ferns, poking around underneath the edge of the house.

"Used to be a spare key right in here somewhere," he said. "Mrs. Sadie always told me that I could use it to get inside should I need to." He panted hard as he worked, and was about to give up when his face lit up with discovery. "Yep! Think this is it."

He yanked his arm out and sat back, holding the prize. It was a tiny, orange Tupperware box, caked with dirt, cracks all around, yet still intact. Marvin popped open the brittle lid and there sat a key.

"Good job!" Donna snatched the key and scampered up the front steps, headed for the door.

"Wait a second, girl!" Marvin said, tumbling up the stairs to the wraparound porch, right behind her. But then his left boot crunched right through one of the rotting planks. "Agghh!"

"Whoa. You okay? Can you pull it out?"

He growled at her haste, then stepped back with his free leg and yanked the boot from a mass of cobwebs, roaches, and rot. "From now on, *I* go first," he instructed, taking the key from her. "The last thing I need is to get hurt out here."

Inside, the foyer and the front room looked untouched. Mustard-colored sheets were draped over scattered furniture. A black telephone sat on a lace-covered end table, and most of the parquet-patterned hardwood floor was covered with a gigantic gold and black Oriental rug.

Donna stood just behind Marvin's right elbow, hesitant to go farther. "Uncle, you think this place is haunted?"

"Hush. There ain't no ghosts in here."

"How do you know?" She spoke in a loud whisper.

"Because I just know," he retorted. "And what are you whispering for?" His niece's girlie ways were getting to him. "C'mon, scout around. Look for magic stuff. You know, things that the church carnival might be able to use."

They poked around the living room, digging through various boxes, piles of magazines and papers that sat in the corner. Marvin tried the glass doorknob of a corner closet, opening it to find yet more stacks of clutter. A handful of fat, outdated neckties hung from the closet pole.

"Here's something!" Donna cried, reaching around him and yanking out a rectangular box from the back of the closet. The front read *Magic for All!* in bright pink letters, right alongside a top hat, a yellow rabbit peeking out from the inside. "Uncle, look at this thing!" The colors resonated through the dust and dimness of the room, but Marvin just grunted and continued picking through the rest of the clutter. Donna flipped the box over to look at the back but in her haste banged it against the overhead shelf, bringing down an avalanche of more boxes, papers, magazines, a cluster of tiny American flags.

"Be careful, girl!" The fallen mess lay at his shins, and he stepped back, letting it crumble to the floor. The last holdout from the shelf suddenly crashed down onto Marvin's feet, a stack of *Missouri Agriculture* magazines, and he cursed and kicked them to the side. A tiny beige pocketknife fell out from the clump of paper, rolled onto the floor.

"Let that be," he barked. "Come on, we need to get upstairs."

He stepped down the hallway, his boots now clicking on the peach-and-black checkered tile which led into the kitchen. At the rear of the kitchen was a door, and Marvin took note that it looked exactly as it had some decades earlier: park-bench green, four boxy patterns just under the door's window, a black screen door just visible through the glass. He shuffled through the kitchen and peered through the large pane, his memory now working overtime.

From the kitchen doorway his niece spoke up. "What's that humming sound?"

He looked out at the back porch, weary of her inquisitiveness. "Nothing. The fridge, probably."

"Uncle!" she belted out. "There's bees in here!"

Red wasps, actually, hundreds of them hovering over a nest the size of a cantaloupe. The nest was up high, attached to the kitchen trim, just over the refrigerator.

"Damnation!" screamed Marvin, holding his hands up in a lame defense. The sudden movement in the room had stirred up the nest, and its defenders circled in fury, some flitting down just over Marvin's flailing arms.

"Uncle, don't move! They won't sting!"

"Whaat?" He kept up his defense and then remembered the door behind him; he turned at a slight angle, fumbling with the doorknob. The wasps were gaining confidence, dozens of them now encircling the space between the nest and Marvin. The doorknob was stiff and resistant and when he at last unlocked it and pulled the door back it stopped short with a swift bang: the safety latch.

"Dammit!" he squealed. He yanked off his cap, waved it back and forth at the wasps as they dropped in larger numbers. "Donna, grab something! Anything! Look for bug spray in the cabinet!"

While she banged around in the pantry he pawed at the latch with one hand but it gave no purchase, stubborn with time. The buzzing grew louder and louder in the tiny kitchen, and he longed for some giant magic wand to wave, extirpate the lot of them. He crouched and put his hands up in an X pattern, just over his face.

"Uncle, hold still! I've found something!"

It was a big red broom, Donna's own version of a magic wand, and as she gripped it tightly, rearing back like Mickey Mantle, her youthfulness and lack of life experience could only elicit one response from her mortified uncle: "No!"

The straw end of the broom whisked through the air, slamming against the cabinets just above the fridge and below the nest. As if in a tornado drill, Marvin covered his head and ran for the kitchen door.

"Go!" he screamed. "Get the hell outta here!" The broom fell to the tile with a thud as Donna turned and also booked it, just ahead of her uncle.

He could hear the swarm just over his head and shoulders, and then there were the stings, one directly on his left elbow, another on his left palm, a third at the top of his right ear. The two stomped out of the kitchen, turned the corner, and raced down the hallway, not knowing where they were going but knowing it wasn't where they were. They came around another corner and came to a stop in a room that resembled a parlor or a lounge. Tattered bed sheets covered a few small sofas, a pair of empty bookcases sat in a corner, and a mish-mash of assorted chairs was strewn throughout the room.

"Those bastards tore me up!" he gasped, looking over his wounds. "What the hell was you thinking?"

"You said to grab something!" She checked over his shoulder, and then stepped to the middle of the room, pulling him by the arm.

"I said to hunt for bug spray. Not a broom! Damnation, Donna." He caught his breath and surveyed the new room.

"Are you okay?"

"Yes," he lied. "No thanks to you." He smeared the back of his wrist across his damp eyebrows, then lightly touched the sting on his ear, wincing. "At least we're in the right place," he went on, motioning to the staircase that sat across the hallway. "*That's* where we need to be."

They stepped quickly up the stairs, waving off a few persistent wasps, the outer guard still in pursuit. Upstairs, the landing was a dark, cherry hardwood, and was littered with small piles of empty hatboxes and bags of folded drapes and blankets. A mop and broom leaned against an old, dilapidated organ that sat in the corner. They found their way to the doorway of the master, and Marvin knew by the positioning of the windows that it was *the* room. His eyes fell across the lime-green carpet, over the room's few belongings, and his only thought was: it's time to pay the piper.

"Uncle, here we are!" She squeezed his throbbing elbow before walking out into the center of the room. "Look at this stuff!"

He gritted his teeth and sucked in the wave of pain that shot up from his elbow. "I have eyes too, you know," he said.

"You think the church could use these in the carnival?" She'd fished a pair of handcuffs from a brown grocery bag teeming with items, and was now trying to squeeze her little wrists through them. "These are what the sheriff carries around on his holster thing!"

There were three dusty sacks sitting on top of a large card table. Marvin watched as Donna rifle through playing cards, red hankies, marbles, sponge balls, dice, a dented top hat, postcards, an armload of knick-knacks and oddities.

"Stop foolin' with all that," he said. "You're missin' the real goods, girl."

He pointed to a tall, flimsy crate that sat in a corner, some of its pine slats barely hanging on. There was stenciled scribble on one side of the crate that he couldn't make out. But the real granddaddy in the room sat just behind the crate, an impressive box some four or five feet high. The sides were lined with wide mahogany planks, fastened tightly at the corners by thin steel plates; a tall glass square, window-like, made up most of the front, framed in by dark-toned wood. The top was covered with a thick square lid, on top of which sat two brass loops, inch-high, which Marvin figured were for padlocks.

His memory jumped to a newspaper clipping he'd seen in his grandmother's scrapbook, some forty years earlier, a snapshot of the great liberator, upside down, in a box that resembled this one. *Did Houdini use this for his show in St. Louis? Or did he have it shipped all the way to rural Missouri, a gift for Sadie?* He wondered what sort of hanky-panky the two had engaged in.

"Uncle," Donna deadpanned, her sight fixed on the massive item. "What in the world is *that*?"

"Not exactly sure." Marvin stepped around the box, running his knuckles across the grooves of the dusty slats, trying to ballpark what it might bring at DeSoto's Auction House. He kneeled down and pushed the corner, ballparking it's weight. Easily over one-hundred pounds, he surmised. No small task. Now eye-level with the lower half of the box, he read a large, red, italicized stamp that told all: *Houdini Enterprises.*

"Uncle, did you hear that?"

"Huh?"

"It sounded like a bump downstairs."

Now that he'd found what he wanted, he was in no mood for childish paranoia. "Come on. We're gonna slide it across the floor."

"Huh? You're gonna take this thing home?"

"You heard me. Let's go."

She stood still, her head cocked sideways, listening for something. "Uncle Marvin, I heard something downstairs."

"You didn't hear a thing," he snapped, stooping behind the box, his hands on the corners. "Now, let's get a move 'on. I'll push the left side and the middle. You take care of the right. It outta slide pretty good across this tight carpet."

And slide it did, like a sled over fresh ice. Marvin was impressed at how fast they got the box over to the doorway; but that was the conclusion of the carpet and the beginning of the bumpy wood floor, the uneven hardwood that comprised most of the upstairs.

He stood for a moment, catching his breath. "Okay, here's what we're gonna do."

"No, here's what *we're* gonna do!"

The voice came from just around the doorway, and it startled Donna so much that she backed against the box, her barrettes clicking against the glass. Two young men stood there, all scowls and frowns. They were rumpled and unshaven, two no-good hoosiers from the backwoods of Missouri. The taller of the two boasted a crowbar while the shorter thug carried a base-ball bat.

"Aw hell," moaned Marvin, "ya'll done snuck up in here right behind us!"

"Shuddup, grandpa," said the tall one, jabbing the crowbar in his face. "Now get over in that corner before I use this thing on you."

Tall boy wore jeans and a green T-shirt, and short boy had on dirty corduroys and a polyester polo shirt; their clothes were dotted with stickers and little brown cockleburs and both of them wore their hair slicked back, glossy wet, which just made them look all the seedier.

"You too, missie," the tall one said, motioning for Donna to move. He patted the side of the box before shooting his partner a greasy grin. "Looks like paw paw and his daughter here came across what we was looking for." His partner nodded and quickly smiled, flashing a row of yellowed, uneven teeth. "C'mon, get 'em over in that corner, Ernest. Use the ropes from those ugly curtains to tie their hands up."

As far as Marvin could tell, the two men weren't carrying any hardware, so he appealed his case. "Aw come on, now. You two don't want to go through with all this."

"Move it, pops," short boy ordered, nudging Marvin's arm with the bat. "Don't make me use this."

He managed to herd them over to the opposite corner of the room and then he had them sit down. He stripped the decorative ropes from the gaudy chartreuse curtains and began tying their hands tight.

Tall boy walked around his new treasure, admiring it, his mule-like grin stretched wide. "Look at what we have here. A real jackpot!" He jabbed his crowbar at Marvin and Donna, who were now bound and secured. "You two sit tight and let us do our work. And no funny business! I wouldn't bother yellin' for help cause ain't nobody around to hear!"

At that, short boy leaned back and howled like a happy drunk, pleased at his work. He slapped a palm across his sticker-ridden britches. And off they went to Houdini's box.

For the better part of fifteen minutes, the two banged and clomped the box across the landing and down the stairs. They fussed and cussed like discharged soldiers, and it burned Marvin up that he'd been duped by two white punks no more organized than a pair of drunk carnies. He sat on the floor in silence, furious at the whole mission. There was then an extremely loud bump, followed up by another round of colorful language, and he knew they were finally downstairs. After a long time, he turned to look at a very liberated Donna.

"What the hell?" he said. "How'd you . . .?"

She beamed from ear to ear while proudly holding up the little beige pocketknife from earlier.

"I didn't say anything but took it when you weren't looking. From the closet downstairs."

My sister is raising a thief, he thought, and began to protest when she shot him a look that read *don't you even.* He just shook his head and looked away. "C'mon, cut me loose."

After nearly five minutes of furious sawing, the rope around his wrists was still not cut. "What's the holdup?" he snapped. "Those two are gonna get away!"

"Yours is tied tighter than mine," she said. "Hang on, I've almost got it."

She worked the blade across the knot like a hand saw, back and forth, quicker and quicker. Just like a woman, Marvin thought miserably. *Slow.* He was still astounded that she'd freed herself, but the fact that she'd beaten him to it just worsened his anger. "Will you hurry it up?"

"Uncle, you're crazy if you're thinking about following them. Those two are dangerous!"

"Dangerous, my foot. Come on, step on it."

The thick knot finally snapped into two and Marvin yanked his hands free, smoothing his fingers over the red imprints on his wrists, wringing them out in the air, as if trying to dry them.

"Okay, listen!" he said. "Here's what we'll do. You stay here, while I go out after them."

"I wanna come," she said, crossing her arms and pursing her little lips.

"You'll do no such thing. This is a man's job, Donna."

"You always say that. And uncle, those white boys weren't much older than me."

"I don't care how old they were," he said, his voice now elevating sharply. "This is serious business. Now, you stay put right here. I'll come back and get you. Aight?"

Donna nodded her head in silence and sat back against the wall, pouting.

On the landing he stopped to listen. Judging by their voices and the ongoing commotion, Marvin guessed the two thugs were somewhere around the front porch.

He grabbed the mop from the corner and treaded down the stairs like a detective. His battle wounds felt even fresher, the stings piercing, his wrists chafed and sore. He'd barely eaten anything all day and now felt the throbbing pangs of hunger. But Marvin Gardner wasn't about to let a couple of kids ruin what was rightfully his, no sir. *I've already been swindled once. It ain't about to happen again.* He reached the bottom floor and he could now hear the two out front, banging his box around, babbling over who was doing most of the work. "Ernest, that ain't tight enough!" *Huh?* "Tie it tighter!" *I am!* The arguing went on, but Marvin was preparing a surprise attack. *I'll go out the kitchen door and run around to the front. Then I'll beat their heads in with this mop handle.*

The orange and black wallpaper, peeling and mildewed, was a jumbled visual mess as he jogged down the hallway, but right as he turned the corner into the kitchen the horror of the wasps tapped his memory's shoulder. They were still there, of course, dozens of them, an angry swirl of winged fighter pilots, and he shrieked like a four-year-old. With his arms up in defense, his legs struggling to hit reverse, Marvin crashed into a table, knocking the hanging kitchen calendar—Colonial Bread's 1968 edition—to the floor. His hands desperately gripped the table's edge and he used it to push off and propel his body out of the room. The hallway now straight ahead, his sight returned to the wallpapered chaos and as he scrambled out the doorway he headed for the first thing he saw: the entrance to the bathroom, directly to his left. Barreling through the doorway, he turned and slammed the door with force, put his back to it and slumped to the floor.

Amidst his gasping and fury, Marvin let loose with another toddler-like scream. But since the bathroom faced the front of the house he quickly reined the noise in, not wanting the two punks to return. He threw his damp Cardinals cap across the ugly turquoise floor, banged his palm against the wall, and commenced to catch his breath.

Stupid wasps, he muttered. He honed in on his hat's sweaty red bill crumpled against the cracked corner tile. *I'll just wait it out.*

The ubiquitous heat of a typical June day in eastern Missouri had faded, blackened by a purple mass of clouds that had rolled in. Out in the yard, the two thieves tied a rope around the box and were now attempting some prehistoric-like maneuver to load it onto the bed of their parked pickup truck. They fought over how to tie the knot, over who should drive the truck, even over whose idea it had been to case the house. The clouds continued to sneak in over the whole of the Robertsville sticks, paired with a tumultuous breeze, perhaps a phantom from a chapter of Missouri history, eager to conceal what went on between Sadie Adams and Mr. Houdini many years earlier.

In the bathroom, Marvin heard a light pecking sound coming from the hallway. As he pressed his ear to the door and listened, he knew it was the wasps. They circled the hallway in aimless fury, lightly flitting and bumping against the top of the door. He would just wait it out. Let the idiot wasps subside. Let Tweedledee and Tweedledum get a little further with their pointless mission, and then launch surprise attack number two.

But then the shots began. Marvin instantly recognized the dry, rapid report as the sounds from his .22 rifle. At the window he shoved Sadie's old vinyl curtains to the side and stared out at the bizarre and the unlikely.

As the shots rang out, tall boy and short boy were taking cover behind the box, heads crouched low, their greasy faces full of terror. Marvin looked to his far right, at the left side of the house, at the upstairs window wide open, at the rectangular strip of lattice that ran down the clapboard siding all the way to the ground. There, on past the corner of the house, sat Donna. Crouched right behind a sun-cracked tire swing, she held Marvin's rifle, the gun's barrel resting on the lower lip of the tire, a little Annie Oakley, firing away. The gunfire skitted through the weeds and saplings, nicking and chipping the corners of the box, pieces of the ancient wood exploding into the air as the two yelped and screamed.

Horrified, Marvin did some screaming of his own. "Hey!" He rapped his knuckles against the glass. "Be careful with my box, Donna! Hey!!" But she was off to the races. She kept at it, a shot here, a shot there, in complete control of the moment.

Tall boy and short boy finally broke for the cab, kicking and scampering through the thick brush. Marvin continued to watch, mesmerized, as Donna picked off the license plate, the tailgate, even the tail lights, the red glass popping and exploding like a jumbo M80 on Independence Day. Above, the canopy of clouds was absolute, a dark, volatile mass that brought soft-slanted sheets of rain across the whole of Robertsville. And as the truck tore away across the bumpy land, Marvin ceased his protest and stood in sweaty disbelief, taking in all of the rural chaos, the rainfall, the wonder of this little girl that was his niece.

***

Back at the house, he threw his feet up on the chipped coffee table and watched his nephew walk around the box in sheer amazement. Marvin's pants were still coated with thorns and burrs and the pain from the stings wasn't letting up. He reached over to the end table for the Calomine and rubbed more lotion over his wounds. Earlier he'd cracked open the sash-and-glass windows of his frame house, allowing a damp breeze to swim through the hallways as the summer downpour raged on.

"I can't get over how cool this thing is!" said Laverne.

Dolores sat in the LaZ Boy, sipping her sweet tea, her eyes still narrowed at her brother. "Cool enough to get killed over?"

Donna sat beside her uncle, yapping the day's events through the phone to a friend. "Dorothy, you shoulda seen the wasps in that house! There was gobs of 'em! Everywhere! No lie!"

Marvin stared at his sister and began a half-baked appeal but she cut him to the quick. "Jes remember the next time you get some hare-brained idea that involves abandoned houses and magic tricks you *call* me before you go draggin' Donna along." She took a swallow of her tea and fanned herself with a *TV Guide*.

"Aw, mama, it wasn't so bad," said Donna, looking up from the phone.

"Do *what*?" cried her mother. "Wasn't so bad??"

But Donna was back to her conversation, now explaining in detail how she had the two crooks at her complete mercy.

"It probably looked a lot better before it got all shot up," said Laverne. There were five or six bullet holes sprayed across the sides of the box, gaping holes encircled by tiny cracks and splintered wood. Two foot-long cracks crept up from the base, a result of tall boy and short boy's careless labor. Laverne ran a thumb across the top of the dusty glass, which was amazingly unharmed, and he stared at the inside of the box.

"I saw a picture of one of these in Aunt Lena's encyclopedia," he said. "I think they would fill this with water and then lower Houdini inside it!" He turned abruptly to his mother. "Mama, I wanna go out to Tillman's Corner and take a look in the old Samuelson house! There might be something old and rare inside!"

"You'll do no such thing."

"But Donna got to go inside Miss Sadie's home!"

"That don't make a darn. Two wrongs don't make a right." She gently rocked back and forth, her eyes still fixed on her brother. "Two wrongs don't *ever* make a right."

Marvin listened to Donna's chipper voice yak on and on, and then he sat back, stared out at the rain dancing down over the Missouri grass, rat-a-tatting across the rusted roof of his chicken house. He turned his gaze to the glass, envisioning the man named Harry Houdini, bound in cuffs, kicking and struggling against the impossible odds to break free. *How did he do such things?*

The scent of the damp Missouri clay swept through the house as the torrid storm came down with even more force. He would have to wait until everything was good and dry before returning the box to Sadie's. Back to where it belonged. He would also need to devise a plan for the wasps.

But for now, he'd decided, it would look good at the Magnolia Springs Baptist Carnival, perhaps something in which children could crawl around and play, little magicians at work. *Step right up! 25 cents to go inside the magic box!* The next great escape artist could hail from right here in east Missouri. That would make both Mr. Houdini and Miss Sadie right proud.

☞ 8

Weezie and the Chimpanzees

The *cheep-cheep* and the *clang-clang* were sounds Louise had recently begun to miss. She remembered how Carson got all giddy over the toy monkey, walking towards the frightened grandchildren as he wound it up, watching them squeal and scream. The memory of the chimpanzee—its red and yellow britches and clean black fur—had recently slammed into Louise one night as she sat and watched one being sold on Antique Discovery, and she wondered what happened to Carson's little monkey.

Finding it might even help with paying off some of the bill.

The *cheep-cheep* and the *clang-clang*, though, were sounds from twenty-five years earlier, long ago. And right now one of those grandkids was living with Louise, proof-positive that there was always something to give life its grind. Always something or somebody that presented a problem. No matter how retired and settled she might be.

Louise stared at the long, ivory-plated hairbrush in her hand, an old family brush she'd just come across. Not needing a stepstool, she reached up and returned the stack of dusty magazines to the top of the closet shelf. She then turned and peered through the crack of her bedroom door, down the span of the parquet-floored hallway, on into the late afternoon haze of the living room where Stuart sat. Short stuff, she silently called him.

Had it really come to this? This situation between her and her shrimp-of-a-grandson? Though Louise's eyesight was still sharp, she adjusted her glasses as she watched him, trying to determine what he was doing, maybe relaxing after his 'part-time job' at Grade A Security. People just aren't hiring anywhere, he says, but when you turn thirty and still haven't developed any meaningful skills, of course people aren't hiring.

She worked the light grey curls back out of her eyes with the brush and finally walked into the living room, her house slippers whisking through the worn carpet. A Spanish textbook sat on the coffee table, right beside a glass of tea and a bowl of Cheetos, the third or fourth time this week. So predictable, Louise thought. She asked him how his shift went.

Stuart was writing something in a little pocket notebook and he put it down with haste, looking up with a smile.

"Oh, fine, Grandma. Nothing exciting, you know." With his sleeves rolled up, he rubbed the big colorful clown on his left arm, something he was always doing. "About the same."

Louise nodded and thought about having a seat on the sofa but decided to remain standing; she looked at the cover of the textbook—*Aquí y Allá*—and then silently bristled as he checked his cell phone. The wet ring created by the glass of tea and the scattered Cheetos crumbs were what really bothered Louise, but she let them go. Mistakes were made, she figured. She looked at the book again.

"Well, don't you have a big test coming up?"

"Oh, yeah." Stuart concentrated on the brush in her hand, as if the bristles could help him remember. "Right, I think so. Big Spanish test. I need to get ready for that one." He picked up the notepad again, opened it, and all Louise could see was a bunch of numbers scrawled out in blue ink.

At five-foot-eleven, Louise towered over her short grandson, and they were a comical sight the few times they were out together in the Kennesaw suburb of Atlanta, at the grocery store or Wal-Mart. He'd moved in for 'only a little while' but he brought his sloppy habits with him. A wet bathroom floor after his shower. The occasional late night on the phone, loud, usually an argument with Lisa, his ex. And yes, those annoying wet glass rings.

Predictable was the best way to describe him. Always saying *yeah* and never *yes ma'am*. Often out late, sleeping in until twelve on his days off. Louise had recently overheard him telling Lisa that he was he was trying to get his life together. But she wasn't sure that was the case. He was perhaps no better than the rest of them. This lot of people that never really got it together.

"Well, I was just looking for those old Spanish cassette tapes I told you about," she said at last. "Thought they might help you with your classes."

"Oh, yeah. The cassette tapes."

"By the way, did you get a chance to look up in the attic?"

"Yeah, I did, Grandma. I did. Had a hard time getting up there. But, yeah, I looked."

"And?"

"Ain't nothing really up there, you know? Bunch of empty boxes and stuff, basically. It wasn't up there."

And that was it. Nothing but junk, he said. Louise nodded and finally plopped down on the old sofa with the black and white shawl draped over the back. Stuart had to go, had errands to run, school items to take care of. He backed his beat-up Ford truck out of the driveway and drove off, and Louise could only speculate if her grandson was going to be on time with next month's rent.

She could use that rent check because of her bills, yes, the bills, *always a damn bill*, Carson used to say. The utilities, groceries, gasoline, and property taxes were usually covered with her modest savings and social security. But there was this new bill that recently had surfaced, a holdover from Carson's horse gambling whims in southern California. Stuart's check would only put a dent in this whopper of a bill. That was, of course, *if* he were able to provide her with one, this grandson of hers who had hit the skids with his girlfriend and moved out of her apartment, his third girlfriend and live-in situation in as many years.

His constant relationship drama was par for the course, one more mess in this mess of a family. Stuart's mom had skipped off to Europe with some French roofer, and his father was on the run from the law, for only God knew what. Louise's only other grandchild, Amber, had recently moved in with a Marine corporal, fresh back from a tour in South Korea, looking for a good time. And good Lord, does anybody get married and stay married anymore?

No, this bill wasn't going anywhere. It was part of the old tracker credit system, something Louise remembered her husband talking about from time to time when he returned from one of his men-only trips out West. It had arrived via a phone call from a young collections idiot. Some boy on his way to becoming a company man without even knowing it.

"We're pretty sure it's the same Carson Snyder, ma'am." His young, smug voice had a nasal whine to it. "He worked for Atlanta Bolt and Fastener, correct?"

Louise took off her glasses and sat down, stunned. "Yes. But . . . there's more than one location, right? There are a lot of employees there, and—"

"Didn't he work for the Airline Drive location? He was employed there in 1974? Resided at 1303 Patsy Lane, Kennesaw, Georgia?"

"Yes, yes," she said, taking an enormous breath. In her head, she did a quick tally of how much money she had in the bank, and then of her monthly budget.

"I'm sorry to tell you this, ma'am. But he's the one."

Trying to fight the bill, Louise used her limited toughness and savvy she'd collected from thirty years of working customer service down at Sears. But it did no good. Everything documented, they said. Here, we can send it to you. His name had been lost within the tracker system, but we came across it and we'd like to settle up. Sure, we can do a payment plan.

The monkey could help pay for a small part of the bill. Louise was no dummy; she'd watched how much the chimpanzee sold for that night on the antique program, both she and Stuart sitting there in silence with a large bowl of Cheetos between them. They talked about the chimpanzee with some nostalgia, how much joy it brought everybody. She hadn't thought of it in so many years. But that night the visual of those bright red and yellow pants and copper cymbals slapped her with ferocity.

A few nights later, while Stuart attempted to cook dinner, she brought up the attic again.

"Grandma, I told you," he said, "I searched every-where up there. I looked not too long after we watched that antique show." A pot of rice was on its way to completion, and the pork chops were slowly frying in one of Louise's forty-year-old pans. "I don't know where that monkey is."

As he stirred the rice, he fixed his eyes on the black and gold emblem of the stove's rear panel, a shiny, lacquered little king holding a pan out in display. Louise reached around Stuart, turning the fire down some, then looked down at his thinning golden-brown hair and his work uniform.

"Sure you checked the whole attic? There's probably a lot of stuff up there."

"Yes, Grandma," he said with a wave of the spatula. "What I saw was a bunch of old Christmas stuff and some empty boxes. That old Frosty that Grandpa used to put out every year."

She remembered that Frosty. Carson had bought it half-price during a January clearance sale at Woolworth's. "Come on, get ready to eat," Stuart said.

They sat, and Louise concentrated on his hair again, fine, light hair, just like Carson's. Stuart's mom would go and on about Stuart's hair when he was a young boy, beaming over her Kool-Aid and magazine. *His hair is so thin and golden, Mom, don't you think? Isn't it?* Louise's eyes fell to Stuart's disheveled uniform, crumpled and unironed, something that seemed to be a pattern with him.

"You, uh," she mumbled, poking at her pork chop with a fork, "you going to have a check for me next week?"

"A check?" His mouth was full and he chewed quickly, glancing at his watch. "Oh, yeah. Yeah. I know I was late last month. But I'm getting more hours at work now. I know you have that big bill you're paying off."

She nodded. "You settle things up with your girlfriend? Uh, your ex-girlfriend?"

"Yeah. Sort of. She keeps asking—she keeps . . ." His voice became soft, and he looked past Louise, at something out the window.

"Asking what?"

"She wants to borrow money. And, well, I just told her I had to start being more responsible. I told her I had to take care of myself first."

Louise worked a sliver of margarine through her rice with a knife and she could suddenly hear the way he sometimes said "What's up dude?" on his phone, loud and stupid. The ridiculous way some young people talked nowadays. Did they have anything else to offer, something fresh or unique?

"I told her this job was good for me, you know? That it helps take my mind off smoking cigarettes, and you know, helps me pay for school. Even though I've got those loans." He held his fork in the air, and assessed it. "She brings me down, grandma. And I've got to be proactive. I need to concentrate on things like my schoolwork."

She brings me down. Louise's mind jumped to the vice-president of the garden club that brought *her* down, one Mrs. Maggie that had an opinion on everything. No, you water the geraniums only twice a week. And lots of shade. Remember: shady ladies. It's the impatiens that you water every other day. *Do you understand?*

Stuart was still talking, but Louise was barely listening. The green and white checkerboard of the tablecloth now coerced her attention, the blur of the cross patterns that gradually led her eyes over to an unfinished novel, *Kramer vs Kramer.* The book was almost buried, hiding under layers of the *Atlanta Journal-Constitution*, and it was stuffed with forgotten garden club papers. Stuart continued to talk while she studied the book's creased spine, still thinking about the garden club, about how much she sometimes wanted to press Maggie's face down into an open bag of potting soil.

***

It eventually became a matter of principle, and that was that. The extra money from selling the toy monkey would help, of course, but Louise knew she would just have to manage. She would have to really watch her spending. No more getting her hair done every other Friday. No more movie matinee after church on Sundays. Easy on the snack aisle at the grocery store. At least for a while.

It was a matter of principle for Louise but it also became a matter of memory. She walked through the house when Stuart was away, tapping the hairbrush in her palm, straining to bring some of those days back. After Carson's death, Louise's daughter had come over and helped clean out all of the clutter and crap in the garage. Power tools, board games. A collection of baseball bats from Carson's youth, chipped and pocked with scratches. A cheap Styrofoam cooler that sat in the corner for decades. There were so many other items. Had they gotten rid of everything, sold it all off? It had been too long.

Louise's daughter might have remembered what happened to the chimpanzee but Louise didn't how to reach her. She was off in Europe, in love, resurrecting her long-gone adolescence. *I think he's the one, Mom!* she'd said, holding a small French dictionary in one hand and a Virginia Slim in the other. Louise asked if she was sure and her daughter just giggled and buried her nose in the dictionary. *Of course I'm sure. Aren't I always?*

Louise's eyes flashed with anger when she thought of her reckless family, of the trickle-down ways of life that engendered irresponsibility. These people did whatever, whenever. At what point do you release your family and let them figure things out on their own? At what point do you stop enabling them?

She stood in Stuart's room, the long-time guest bedroom. Everybody stayed in this room, out-of-town friends, family; the same Samsonite luggage sat heavy and dusty in the closet, crammed in alongside hatboxes, an unopened box of moth balls, a stack of aging garden club brochures.

But there was now a new reality, the blur of blue jeans and rock n roll T-shirts across the floor and bed, the sweaty smell of careless youth that permeated her once-clean guest room. On the dresser lay a pink cigarette lighter, movie ticket stubs, a *Jurassic Park* novel, and a pocketknife. She sat on the edge of the unmade bed, studying the small knife. The words *old timer* were etched into the mahogany-toned handle.

This was the same dresser that Carson became angry over when Louise and a friend brought it home one day after antique shopping. Louise had never dared to lash back at her husband the way she sometimes wanted. That just really wasn't done back then, she reflected, the way her daughter now did to a boyfriend over a parking spot or the failure to pay a bill, such a thing the gradual product of women's liberation and all that. Despite Carson's rare bossy ways and the problems his gambling vices had brought her, there was never a time that Louise *didn't* miss him. His strong, protective presence, the way he affectionately called her Weezie.

But since his death she'd thought more and more about the subtle oppression of those times. The days in which men *made all of the decisions*, as her daughter was prone to say with such extraordinary venom.

Of course, there were women, too, women who picked and nagged. Those know-it-all PTA types with commanding personalities; her bossy neighbor, Rudell, who often controlled their fence-line conversations so that Louise could barely get a word in. Maggie, at the garden club meetings, who delegated tasks to everybody but herself.

Louise reached out with the knife—now open—and tapped the blade on the dresser's mirror twice. She then studied herself in the reflection, her long arms, her jaw, still firm and even. She tapped the glass again, then dropped the knife into her pocket and walked out, angry at herself for stewing in such hopeless fury. *Why all of these thoughts now, at seventy-two?* Is it time to make changes?

She was old, she figured. Let it go, let live. Stuart can still become an adult, she told herself out loud one morning while putting on her bathrobe, running the ivory brush through her hair. And even though he's in there burning the bacon and probably making weak coffee, short-stuff, he's still up before me. About to go to work. That's good for something.

"Good morning, Grandma. Have some coffee?"

Louise nodded, and in her morning slippers padded her way to the table and sat down. She glanced at his uniform, didn't need her glasses to see it was crinkled and dusty. "You're up early. Early shift today?"

"Yeah, I've gotta go in at eight. They're finally giving me more hours."

She wrapped her long fingers around the warm cup and continued to assess Stuart's untucked shirt and wrinkled pants. She wondered how good he'd be in a physical confrontation. *Here I go again.* Do other grandmothers think this way about their own grandchildren?

"You know, I was thinking," he said, his brown eyes just over the spatula that he held up. "Mom had several big yard sales right after Grandpa died, and you weren't always here for them."

"Where was I?"

"Not sure. I remember, though, us out front getting rid of stuff and you weren't around."

Louise looked down into her cup, concentrating hard, some of those forgotten days coming back to her. All of the compressed clutter and junk she'd become so weary of.

Stuart slid a plate of grits and bacon across the checkered tablecloth to Louise. "Uh, Grandma?"

"Yes?"

"Have you been in my room?"

It registered with Louise right away that it was the first time she'd ever lied to her grandson. She arranged the plate in front of her. "No, hon. What do you mean?"

Stuart raked his fingers across his tattoo and sat down, looking confused. "Oh, nothing. Thought that maybe you were cleaning up in there, that's all. I know it sort of needs it."

Louise suddenly raised her eyebrows. "Well, that's putting it mildly," she said, tasting her grits and rapidly maintaining the natural pace of conversation. "Your room does need cleaning."

"Right. I know it does." He squared his plate in front of him, pulled his chair up to the table, looking shorter than ever, she determined.

"I mean, you know, it could *use* a good cleaning. That's what I'm trying to say," she said.

"I know."

She stirred her food and then studied the fleck of grits on her left knuckle, taking her train of thought elsewhere. She then looked up and watched Stuart slop grits across his chin, down onto the edge of his plate, and it suddenly hit Louise that he had sat here at the dining room table with her no more than a couple of dozen times, total. Who was this grandson of hers?

"I'll try and be neater," Stuart said, crunching the bacon vigorously as he chewed. "I promise."

Louise smiled weakly, not knowing what to say. The smell of overcooked bacon hovered through the dining room, and she glanced over at her novel, now half-hidden behind a jar of malt, more newspapers, a bag of chips. The edge of the garden club papers were sticking out of the end of the book, the green ink of the scribbled hierarchy of power and responsibilities barely visible.

"I want to make you proud," Stuart said, pushing away his plate and pulling his sleeves down, buttoning his cuffs. "You know that, right?"

She nodded.

"I gotta go, though. I can't be late. My boss might be looking at me for night shift, which would be full-time."

"Well, good."

"I told these jokers I had bills to pay," he said with a big smile, and Louise wondered whether such a statement made him proud. "I need those hours!"

He got up to leave and Louise slid her fingers across the green-and-white blocks of the tablecloth pattern, reaching for the forgotten novel. She chewed her breakfast as she pulled the papers out and set them aside, languidly thumbing through the musty pages of the book.

***

Louise had never abused her height, the psychological advantage she learned it could potentially give her in moments of disagreement. She knew of the subtle advantages in being tall, and she sometimes lay in bed at night, thinking of the many encounters in which she didn't utilize this asset. She climbed up another two rungs on the ladder, then caught herself stepping back down to see if she'd really heard Stuart's car pull into the carport. But then, what did it matter? *Isn't this my house?*

Louise couldn't remember the last time she'd been on a ladder. Ten, maybe twenty years, she surmised. But there was the third, no, now fourth rung, and the attic panel door was now right at her face, a dusty, off-white square, lightly covered in cobwebs. Louise did not look down: she kept her old Adidas yard shoes squarely rooted on this rung and gently pushed up on the panel. There was no stick or resistance, and she slid the door easily over to the side, stared up through the dark heat directly above, the little parallel lines of light faintly glowing in the attic ceiling. She carefully stepped up one more rung and was now shoulder-level with the attic floor. The heat and stale air seized her, forcing a few coughs.

There had been *two* monkeys, a forgotten fact that slammed into her earlier that morning as she pored over an old diary, squinting at the faded pencil etching. *Lovie's brought two wind-up chimpanzees back from Las Vegas!* The handwriting of those days whipped through her mind like a desert wind, bringing back a bold visual of Carson standing there in the carport, pulling out a large shopping bag from the trunk of his old Chevy. The heat of the attic was intense, the funk of old insulation and of rodents long dead. She took another slow, solid step in her green Adidas, shoes she normally wore when gardening. Her right hand was locked to the inside frame of the panel opening and with her left she gingerly fished the junk-drawer flashlight from her front pocket.

No, taking advantage of her height was not something that Louise desired. But there were so many times in which it could have been used. She held the flashlight firmly and turned her body, periscoping the light's pale stretch across the attic floor, over the small piles of Christmas tinsel, clumps of insulation, a faded Frosty who'd seen better days. And there, right at the conclusion of the beam's full circle, sat two blue and white boxes. They leaped right out at her, slapping her memory, bringing back 1980 all over again.

"Weezie, look at what I brought you," Carson had said, howling, a chimpanzee in each hand, both of them cheeping and clanging away. She jumped back against the screen door, mortified but then amused. The tight black fur of the monkeys looked scrubbed and clean, and though they were entertaining, the little chimps gave her the willies, she'd told him.

She looked at the boxes for another moment, the memory of the cardboard's crisp colors soaking through her. The fact that they were not coated in dust and neatly placed only a few feet from the attic door was all that Louise needed to know.

***

To Louise, so many people made life more challenging than necessary. People who tried to short-cut
life but in the process walked all over others. The
young, arrogant, collections clerk. Her son-in-law, Stuart's father, a worthless Yankee, with that stupid,
exaggerated accent, so pretentiously tough. He was a
typical man from the North, Louise thought, always
trying to control the conversation the few times they all
dined together. *Carson, that may have been the way it's
done in Georgia. But in Connecticut we do it different.
You take architecture, for example* . . . And there he
went, rambling on over his corned beef and carrots,
making sure everybody was making eye-contact with
him as he yapped.

What did a plumber from Connecticut know? Especially now, since he was in trouble, on the run. And
indeed, what *did* a plumber from Connecticut know? It
was no wonder Stuart wasn't going anywhere.

It wasn't that Louise had begun to hate certain people, or even those in authority. No. She was certainly
teachable and mindful of people's roles. And she was
excessively patient. Late one afternoon, she sat back in
the flowerbed of the subdivision entrance, stopping her
work and considering this strength of hers. How she
constantly let Rudell control the pace of their fence-

line conversations. The way she deferred to Mrs. Maggie and her lectures on planting ferns. *Keep them in the back, plant them behind the impatiens for full effect. Understand?*

She glanced down at her work, the shimmering array of the flowerbed's green, lavender, and blue colors, wonderfully layered, as crisp as a laser. Louise felt accomplished, productive.

Some people just overstep their boundaries, she confirmed to herself, pulling off her gloves and inspecting her Adidas. That's all. Some people think everybody but them is stupid.

"Look at that pretty lady."

Louise looked up, startled. Stuart had just pulled into the entrance and came to a stop; the passenger-side window was rolled down, and he stared at her across the seat, grinning.

"Looks good!" he called out. "Mom never told us you had such a green thumb."

His sleeves were rolled up on his work shirt, and with his big jumbo clown exposed he looked happy and ridiculous. Why is it, she thought, that so many people that have tattoos are the ones who can least afford them?

"Well . . ." she said.

"And don't be modest. You do a lot more than most people your age do."

Louise spotted the pack of cigarettes squashed between the windshield and the dashboard, and then she noticed the front tire had finally given in, in its place a lowly spare. "Have a flat tire, hon?"

"Actually, yeah. I had a pretty rotten morning. It finally went out," he said, pointing across the seat to the front of the car. "That's the spare now, but I'll have to get a new one. But it's okay. Soon my job should be giving me even more hours, and I'll be making more money!" He said this last part with a shrug and a smile.

"Well. Maybe we can get it fixed for you."

He leaned back into his driver's position. "Hey, don't be too late getting home. I'm gonna have a surprise for you tonight, Grandma. You're gonna love it."

She watched his truck scuttle away, and then right behind him pulled in Rudell, in her still-immaculate Fifth Avenue; she frantically waved at Louise as if they hadn't seen each other in years. Louise stared back, wiping her damp forehead, then returned a slight nod to her neighbor.

***

It was a brisk and windy evening, unusually cool and not humid for April in north Georgia. Louise got up to close some of the windows she'd opened earlier.

It was well past midnight, but she'd never really fallen asleep. In the living room she came to a stop, looking around for her glasses, but then remembered that she didn't need them. The steady, wooden click of the old grandfather clock resounded softly, and she walked over to the long, thin mirror hanging in the corner of the room.

Five-foot-eleven, ramrod straight, still steady and strong. This was the body that spent decades and decades cooking and cleaning, paying bills, holding down full-time work at Sears. This slender, able body had mounted that rickety ladder, climbed into the attic. She turned, padded over to the dining room table. A small coconut cake—her favorite—was encased in her old Tupperware container, which sat beside the *Kramer vs. Kramer* novel and the ivory-plated brush. She pulled the garden club papers out of the book, threw them into the trash, and then picked up her hairbrush.

Louise stood in the cool blackness of the hallway shadows, statue-still. As she clicked her nails on the slick back of the brush, the brisk breeze blew in from the other open windows, dancing through the house. Holding the brush firmly, she stepped towards her grandson's bedroom.

The little hallway nightlight pushed a faint beam through the cracked doorway, the light stretching across Stuart's bed; his clown peered right up at Louise, its yellow and cream face standing watch. The spring wind tumbled through the bedroom, ruffling the old curtains, and Louise loomed over Stuart's bed, tall, strong and proud. She reached down to run a hand over the top of the bedspread, smoothing it out, pulling it up to his chin. He'd always been a heavy sleeper. She reached down with her other hand.

Did you really think that making my favorite cake was going to change things? This was the same five-foot-eleven body that escorted her daughter's girl scout troop on camping trips, saying "sure, okay" to the other aggressive and organized mothers, those do-it-all moms that went overboard on such outings. The same body that once backed off and took the high road when Rudell stood at the backyard fence-line, defiant, lawyer-like, charging that the large roots of Louise's trees pushing their way through the fence were an invasion of Rudell's yard space. And it was the same body that had to put up with people that made reckless, inconsiderate choices.

Louise ran her long fingers through Stuart's stringy bangs the way she used to with Carson's beautiful hair while he slept. *Cheep-cheep, clang-clang.* The monkeys would look good placed on the dresser in the other bedroom. Or maybe in this bedroom once Stuart was gone. The nightlight pushed forth a stretch of warm light across his face, and when he opened his eyes, wide and petrified, his face became even more pronounced with the light.

"Grandma. Grandma, what are you doing?"

He gasped, eyes stretched even wider, and his grandmother smiled down at him, letting her fingernails sift through the tips of his bangs one last time. *You need more hours at work, my foot.* This was the same body that lorded over a customer earlier that day at the market, a man who reached for the last two ripe nectarines but was cut off by Louise's long arm, snatching them up as she shot a quick stare down at the confused little man. *Miss? Excuse me, Miss, but I had those first? Miss?*

Yes, the monkeys would indeed look good in one of the bedrooms, the threadbare sweaters still clinging to tired shoulders that worked those old copper cymbals. The monkey's shoulders may have been slightly hunched over but they were still tall and proud. Oh yes, Louise thought, staring down at Stuart's chalky, still face. Tall, strong, and proud.

☛ 9

Bonnie and Grambling

It was said that upon being shot she screeched like a panther. As Keith stood and read the old iron plaque, he thought about how bloodcurdling those screams must have sounded soaring through the Louisiana forest. Highway 154 was a two–laner that cut a swath through the surrounding willows and pines but Keith had yet to see another car; there was just the hot breeze that occasionally stirred the soft air, kicking up the sweet stench of pine needles and dirt. But there hadn't always been the peace of this little moment. He trembled at the sudden visual of the thick blood that once stained the grass and dirt in front of him.

Back at the car, Jackie had her feet up on the dashboard. Her headphones were turned all the way up to Eminem, someone her middle-aged father had only barely heard of. As Keith swung back into the driver seat, she looked at him.

"What were you counting out there?"

He tossed his pocket notebook and pen up on the dash and backed the car out of the little pebbles-and-dirt pull-off. "You could hear that?" he asked. It was midday in Gibsland, Louisiana, and their next point of destination was Grambling State University, about twenty-five miles away. A quartet of ugly vultures circled overhead nearby, lowering in for their lunch.

"Yeah, you were counting something as you walked." She peered out at the vultures and then curled her tongue, snake-like, flashing her piercing. Her music seemed to get louder and louder, but she didn't bother turning it down. "What were you doing?"

She always had excellent hearing, he remembered, something that he and his wife were told every year when the state's board of health came to the school district and gave each child visual and hearing tests. *Girl could hear a cow mooing over in the next county*, Keith's brother would say whenever Jackie went to stay with him for a few weeks every summer, way out in Kaufman County.

"I was just counting the steps off from that memorial plaque they erected," he said with a quick smile, shoving his stringy black hair back off his forehead. "Some historians claim they were actually murdered about fifteen feet from where the plaque stands. There's an ongoing debate. I wanted to see for myself, I guess."

The car picked up acceleration and shot down the empty county highway. Keith wasn't sure how much interest his eighteen-year-old daughter now had in history but he could hope. Jackie was back to bouncing her head to the music, though he knew she'd heard him.

"That's . . . like, creepy," she said, adjusting her bare feet on the dashboard. "Like seriously, creepy."

She pulled her belly shirt down over her navel, staring out at the clumps of eastern leatherwood shrubbery and the scattered blackberries.

"Come on, it's history. It's cool."

He was happy they were having this little exchange. Jackie had been silent for most of the four-hour drive from Dallas, an obvious consequence of having spent very little time with her father in the pre-vious two years since the divorce. This was partly because Keith now lived and taught college in Denton, a good forty miles north of Dallas. But most of their time apart, Keith was convinced, could be blamed on the complicated rage and spontaneous lifestyle of Alda, his ex-wife.

"History, right?" he asked. "You used to love it. Going over the presidents and all of those oddball facts. Who was born where, who did what."

The fury of Eminem was now louder, pounding its way through the headphones, but she still nodded with a slight smile. "Yeah. It was cool. And then Mom would come in and try to change the conversation." Her wispy blond bangs danced against her forehead as she bobbed to the beat. "George Washington and Ches-ter Arthur, the only two men to be sworn-in in New York City. Millard Fillmore: the most forgotten presi-dent."

"Right! And do you remember what I taught you about Woodrow Wilson?"

"Only president to earn a PhD. Only person to be the governor of New Jersey and the president of Prince-ton before becoming president of the United States." She looked numb and bored, as if she'd just went over the facts the day before. "But you know what, Dad?"

"What?" Keith suddenly longed for those evenings spent together by the fireplace during the north Texas winters, reciting historical tidbits, dates and birth-places; even Alda would sometimes join in on the trivia, sipping hot chocolate, her arm around Jackie. Family, simplicity. The way it all ought to be.

"That was a long time ago."

"Yes. I guess it was," he said flatly. A few years for a teenager were like a few minutes for someone his age, he thought. "Enough time to forget some things."

"Enough time to forget a lot of things."

He gave her a quick sidelong look, slowly nodded his head. The car stayed within the dotted lines of the warm asphalt, lurching left to right around the sharp curves. Keith took sudden notice that there really *was* nothing out here in this forgotten, forlorn part of the parish, and the macabre gun-down of the famous pair was now all around him, the blurry sight of the bloody bodies of Bonnie and Clyde swimming through the dusty windshield. Jackie was right: this *was* creepy. His daughter had gone through so much and he pondered the wisdom in bringing her out here. And then he remembered there were things he needed to ask her.

***

Keith had had his fun, and hadn't always done his best to remain in contact with Jackie. Being single again had led to flirting with graduate students and attending university faculty parties. Hanging out on Denton's Frye Street with the young campus bohemians, trying to play the part. Best of all, there was the sheer liberation from the unpredictable chaos of Alda.

But his ex-wife, true to form, liked playing the cruel game. She decided when Keith could see their daughter. She called the shots, and Keith, not having the unending fortitude that Alda possessed, didn't try to fight it. *I don't give up on anything* was something she was proud of saying. And after the divorce, her single lifestyle was something she became proud of, this new odyssey, a way of obtaining *what I never got to experience.* Keith would discover that Alda was frequenting the all-night warehouse raves in downtown Dallas, as well as the underground weekend racing scene, out in the backfields of nearby Mineral Wells, coming home intoxicated, long past midnight.

"You're neglecting some of the most precious years of your daughter's life," Keith once told her. *She's your daughter too*, Alda countered, in one of their many telephone arguments. "And I'll do things any way I damn well please." Her rage and her new lifestyle went on, and the distance between her and Keith widened.

Much of the remaining drive to the campus was spent in silence. They drove through Gibsland proper and then got on Highway 80, yet another chipped two-laner that snaked through the thick Louisiana woods and gradually found its way to Grambling State University. Keith pulled up to the front of the school and parked in the admissions office lot.

In recent years Jackie had expressed an interest in attending the college. Several of her friends from high school were now students there, and Keith was leery of the hip-hop lifestyle Jackie had taken to since making those friends. She wore corn rows in her hair, picked up pieces of edgy slang. And the music she listened to, Keith told everybody, was so loud and pernicious that it made you question whether it *was* music.

He looked over at his daughter, who already had her hand on the door handle.

"Sure you're going to be okay?"

"I'm fine, Dad. I'm just gonna walk around for a little while, do a little tour with one of the counselors. Plus, I have friends here." She closed the door and stared at him through the open window. "You know that."

"You sure you don't want company?"

"You remember the rules, Dad. I do this by myself."

It was already past one, so she didn't have but a few hours before they had to head back. He sat in the parking lot humidity, grading a handful of freshman history exams, looking up now and again, thinking about his teenage daughter alone on a university campus. *How would I have fared at that age, walking around by myself, surrounded by college students? Would I have been as independent and as able?*

It was hard enough to see his daughter regularly. Since Alda's death five months earlier, Jackie had been staying with her aunt in Dallas, finishing out the last of her senior year. And even if he had lived closer, Keith wasn't sure that she would have chosen to live with him. He tried more than once, driving down to Dallas on weekends to take her out for ice cream, his attempts at communication usually met with a frosty silence. Jackie's days had become busy, preparing for the prom, spring fever. Her own liberation from the shackles of her mother's psychological warfare.

Would he have had such maturity and boldness? Such fortitude? And just how would he react if he'd found his own mother hanging from her bedroom ceiling fan?

A couple of hours passed, and Keith dozed off with the radio on, dreaming that he was spying on Alda at some Fort Worth strip club as she danced for several men. When she noticed Keith in the back of the bar she ran over to him, her green thong glowing in the flashing lights, and unloaded her venom, screaming. The whole time Jackie sat outside in the car, exposed, Keith felt, to so much garbage, so much base behavior.

Waves of gray and hot columns of light inundated Keith throughout his next dream, in which he was being wakened by Jackie, who was crying, telling him the news of Alda. As Jackie's aunt led her away, sobbing, Keith could see the blur of blue lights in the background. He could hear the officers on their radio mikes, talking about the body and how they were going to take it down.

He woke up quickly to the slamming of the door; he sat up, the backdrop of the bland campus and the dim, gray air bringing him back. Jackie was right there, happy, a big grin.

"Okay, let's roll. I'm done."

What's she been doing? he wondered. A few of the exams fell from his lap to the floorboard, and Keith grunted while reaching down to get them, his damp, mop-like hair falling over his pale forehead and face.

"What's wrong?" she asked. "Did I scare you?"

He knew she liked the campus because she was all smiles, her tongue ring catching some of the day's waning sunlight. He said no, he was okay, was just trying to wake up. Keith started the ignition and watched his daughter play with her cell phone and then put her headphones back on.

They exited the campus, the car coasting past the outdated buildings and dorms. Keith wondered about the impending house parties and college life out here, out in the middle of nowhere. Why attend a school 240 miles from Dallas, her home? Why here? An old barbecue shack, beckoning to hungry truckers, stood near the ramp exit as the car accelerated back on to I-20 for the long haul home. He took quick notice of a faded, flimsy plywood sign advertising the *Bonnie and Clyde Museum! 15 Miles Ahead!*

Keith suddenly simmered with anger and disgust at haven taken advantage of the trip to quench his undying lust for history. And moreover, he was awakening to the brutal reality of just how much two years of little communication had taken its toll. Keith needed his daughter to know he was there for her, that he was sorry he hadn't gotten her out of Alda's home sooner.

He cleared his throat and slowly turned his head to Jackie. But she was already talking.

"You know, Dad, we could maybe do something for Halloween."

"What do you mean?"

"You know, this whole Bonnie and Clyde thing you're in love with. I could come home from college, and we could get dressed up and go out." She fiddled with her cell and scratched her arm. "I don't know, maybe go to a Halloween party or something."

He liked this idea. If he and Jackie ever became close again they could be the modern day Bonnie and Clyde. The father-and-daughter equivalent. A more beneficent pair, he mused, driving around and robbing banks. Giving the money to the Smithsonian or to the needy Bonnie and Clyde museum.

What a stupid idea, he thought. There were other things far more important than putting on Halloween costumes. "Look. I need to ask you something."

Jackie didn't turn off the music or pull off her headphones but instead just glared at him, maybe disappointed at the interruption in her attempt at happy conversation. Her head remained firmly planted back against the headrest. "What?"

"How long . . . how long did your mother, like . . . *suffer?*"

"Excuse me? You're really asking me this?"

"No. Not *that*," Keith said quickly. "Not when you, um, found her." He made sure their eyes met. "No, I mean, do you think she was really depressed?"

He'd forgotten just how deep the almond texture of his daughter's eyes was, rich and fluid, and he then noticed how the glint of her tongue piercing—something he was still getting used to—actually complemented the color of her eyes.

Eminem's voice continued to bump and hit, but Jackie's eyes were now locked to the windshield, straight ahead. "I don't know. I didn't see her very much. Towards the end. We just weren't talking."

"Why not?" He had to be careful.

"Mom didn't approve of my music. You know, my hip-hop music." She pointed flippantly at her headphones. "Or the kinds of friends I hung out with. People in general."

People to Keith meant hanging out with older boys, the wrong crowd at the wrong age. He'd been filled in by her neighbors and by some of the parents at Jackie's high school. He had ideas. *People.*

"Well, here's what I'm getting at: do you think she needed . . . help?"

"Help?"

"Yes. Could we have gotten her some, you know, professional help? And maybe gotten you out of there?" He hated that it sounded so after-the-fact.

"Oh, Dad. Who knows? Everybody needs help *after* they're gone, right? Once we figure all that out it's too late. I stopped trying to figure out Mom years ago."

Keith let this sink in, marveling at the wisdom of his daughter, a girl still in high school. And there was satisfaction: she now knew her father would have done more if he'd known how grave everything was. He would have done anything, Keith affirmed to himself. An eighteen-wheeler roared by, crunchy clods of dirt sticking to the rims of the tires as they spun, and he switched on his lights. Dusk was dropping across the fields and forests of western Louisiana, and the highway stripes were harder to make out. He looked carefully at her, the guilt still heavy.

"Jackie, I want to ask you something else." He paced himself, remembering the words of the psychologist. *Go easy, approach it casually but with love. You're still her father.* "You know that we haven't ever talked about this. But you . . . you were the one that found her. Right?"

She told him that she did, and this shook Keith. He attempted to block any emotion, visually replacing her with one of his failing students that sometimes came to his office, the usual sob-story of how they just weren't able to study for the mid-term.

"I can't even begin to imagine. I . . . Jackie, I just need to make sure you're okay. That's all. You don't know how worried I've been about you."

She was silent, absolutely motionless, and Keith became so terrified that he'd resurrected an image that needed to stay interred that he quickly moved on.

"Your mother was, well, behaving erratically, wasn't she?" he asked. "I mean, she was partying, right?"

"Yeah, Dad. Partying—ha. It was beyond partying. When you're about to lose your house, and you're smoking weed almost every day and hanging out with every guitar player you meet online, I'd say so. Is that partying enough for you? She partied until it drove her into doing what she did."

It was his turn to become silent. He fixed his vision on the dimming highway, allowing the fresh visuals of Alda to sink in. Then, though he fought it, another thought squeezed its way in sideways. After the ambush, one of the parish lawmen tried to saw off the trigger finger of the deceased Bonnie, a keepsake souvenir for posterity. Or maybe even for money. *How dominant was the this-could-one-day-be-valuable mindset in rural Louisiana of the 1930s?* Another stupid idea, he thought.

Jackie seemed to be on a roll. "And yeah, I found her. Heck, I was home when she did it."

"Wait." His thoughts froze, all at once. "You were home?"

"Of course. I was in my bedroom, down the hall."

Keith's eyes fell across the multitude of roadside pines, skimming over the scratches and dust marks of the windshield glass. New things were happening here.

"Anything else, Dad? I don't like thinking about it. We weren't getting along, you know. It wasn't good. She had her issues."

"Hon, I didn't know that you were—"

"It was just like any other day," Jackie said, now almost gushing, picking up her words with more momentum. "I was supposed to go to the movies, and I didn't."

"That's what I don't get. I thought you went to the movies," Keith said, thinking back to the horrible haze of the hours just after he'd talked to the police and found out. He remembered seeing or hearing the word *movies* but overall he'd blocked the details and specifics out, the tragedy as excruciating as it was. All he'd been concerned with was his daughter's safety.

They caught up to the truck, and its dirty metallic blur was right there, just outside the window. It rattled his memory of the whole event, annoying him.

"No. I didn't go to the movies. I had a huge headache so I just stayed home and read."

"You read?"

"I didn't feel like hearing or watching anything. So I read, of all things. I played my music and read that

Wacky Presidential Facts book you brought me from Washington." The carnal pounding of the bass and the beat of Eminem was now pushing its way through the headphones, louder than ever. She looked out at the eighteen-wheeler, zipping alongside them, a mutilated Gore-Lieberman sticker clinging to the weathered side. Keith wanted to press on, needed to press on, but she was already talking.

"She was in there, in her room. Talking, you know, in a hushed voice, to somebody on her phone. Probably one of her ten boyfriends."

Jackie kept talking but he interrupted and asked her how she knew that.

"Dad, it was freakin' obvious. I could hear her. She was always in there, whispering to somebody, or some dude about something."

Her voice had risen, was now quivering, and Keith knew he didn't have long.

"And, you know, I was lying there, reading. And that was it. That . . ." She was shaking her head and staring at the truck, now several car lengths ahead of them, it's explosive trail of wind whipping through their open windows. Keith strained to hear his daughter but she was done. She put her head back and closed her eyes, the music quiet for a moment, a new song about to begin.

He took an enormous breath. "So Jackie, would you like—"

"I'd like to stop talking about it is what I'd like to do." The deep bass and electronic hook of the next song began. With her eyes still closed, she turned up the music even louder.

The car steadied down I-20 across the state line. The ubiquitous heat from the asphalt slowly seeped up into the evening, easing across the fields of cattle and the faded, forgotten billboards. Keith watched the last seconds of the sky's thick maroon rim press down across the horizon. He thought of the way he'd earlier salivated over getting back to the history department and bragging about visiting the memorial. Showing off the pictures of the plaque, the spookiness of the wooded area. As his Nissan hit eighty the rim of the horizon now morphed into a crossover of maroon and black, and though he listened with pleasure to the soft breaths of Jackie's slumber, his hands trembled lightly on the steering wheel.

After we left, did another obsessed bookworm pull off the road and take a long look at the historical marker? Yet another imbecilic idea. He decided that, no, the site had remained free of visitors for the remainder of the day. His front porch, though, had been full of visitors that Halloween night so many years ago, the trick-or-treaters milling across the front porch. Jackie was dressed as Little Bo Peep, her plastic yellow cane leaning in the bedroom corner after she finally went to bed, exhausted. Keith welcomed this new distraction. Yet he pushed his thin, damp hair off his forehead, sick of the southern heat, disgusted with so many thoughts and too many memories.

The ugly terror of what happened in Gibsland in 1934 would always arouse his senses. For Halloween, they *could* dress up like the old outlaws, he decided. Keith and his tommy-gun, Jackie with her blood-splattered dress and hand revolver. It would be a big move, a bold step on the path back to a better relationship. But there was something more powerful than the lingering bloody visual of the hapless duo or the happy thought of a Halloween spent with his daughter. There was Keith's newfound concern over whether Jackie had had the opportunity to stop her mother from taking her life.

☛ 10

God Bless Leatherface

C hase stooped low, angling his camera in order to get a better snapshot of the weathered clapboard that stretched down the side of the old farmhouse. The clapboard siding ran all the way from the sun-ripped shingles to the chipped foundation. He passed the camera to LaMonica, then walked to the corner of the house, still amazed at the absence of tourist graffiti, of any *Jackie loves Jake* such scrawling. The air was calm and still, the Texas heat unrelenting even at four in the afternoon. As he turned the corner he stopped to absorb the surrounding acres of dry grass, chaparral and pecan trees, wondering if those screams from 1974 were still out there, soaked up by the Texas wilderness.

He stared out at their van, parked some fifty yards from the house, sitting amidst the tall scrub brush of the one-time driveway. For the first time the parallel of the two vans hit him, one from the movie, the other one right here and now. The thought brought a light smile. He quickly scanned the large yard, left to right. Bruce and Candy were nowhere in sight.

"Where's your uncle and what's-her-face?" he asked LaMonica.

"Who knows?" she said, moving in for a close-up of one of the window's ripped screens. "Bruce said he had to take a leak. He's probably walking around, looking for a perfect spot to christen this freaky place. It sure as hell needs it." She laughed, then clicked the camera's button several times.

"He didn't go inside the house, did he?"

"I don't know, Chase." She lowered the camera and looked at him. "I don't think so. What are you worried about him for?"

"We've just got to be careful," he replied, shielding his eyes with both hands as he checked the front yard again, and then the edge of the woods. "You read that big sign."

Right at the grassy turnoff from the county highway was a giant piece of plywood, nailed to two old posts, painted white. Its peeling red letters read *KEEP OUT OR GO TO JAIL. OR WORSE.*

"He'll be fine," she said, now walking past him, steadying the camera for a shot of the front porch. "Anyway, relax. We won't be here long."

He quickly walked to catch up with her. "Thanks for taking so many pictures. I never even thought about bringing a camera."

"That's because you're a MBA geek. All you people think about is money, not art." She kneeled down and snapped a side shot of the porch's railing, caked with cobwebs, the paint of each spindle reduced to an alligator-skin crackle.

"And this MBA geek will own the company that you'll one day try and get a job with." He suddenly headed for the front steps. "Let's check out the inside."

"Don't you want to go look for the bones?"

"We will in a minute. Come on. Let's go in first."

The house's foyer instantly regurgitated visuals of the movie for Chase, images of Marilyn Burns—the screaming blonde protagonist—racing up the staircase, fleeing from the chainsaw-wielding maniac. A rickety chandelier hung from above, most of its glass pendants long gone. Tiny pieces of masking tape in X patterns, worn to threads, dotted the corners of the floor. They stepped carefully into the next room. Large sheets of butcher paper—most of it curled up at the edges—were still taped over much of the faded flowered wallpaper that met the wainscoting in the middle of the wall. The old hardwood floor creaked with age. But the rooms were amazingly clean and empty, with very little sign of vandalism or tourist activity.

"This was the dining room," Chase said, coming to a stop, assessing the room's size, his mind darting back to the comical yet disturbing scene in which Grandpa, Leatherface, and the rest of the family all sat around the dinner table, taunting the tied-up blonde.

On the table were small piles of bird feathers and scattered chicken bones, some of which Chase hoped were still here, neatly tucked away amidst the branches of the only red oak in the surrounding area.

"This really creeps me out," LaMonica said, walking over to a window.

"You keep saying that. You never even saw the movie."

"But I've heard you talk about it for years. I know about this room. A backwoods family sitting around the table, torturing a sorority bimbo that's tied up." As she talked she pointed around the room, jabbing at the film's characters, as if they were still there.

He ran his fingers across the yellowed butcher paper and grinned, the full impact of where they actually were finally hitting him. He'd first watched the *Texas Chainsaw Massacre* when he was ten, via the breadmaker-sized VCR at Leslie Kraft's house, and the film's rural horror had enthralled him, creating the longing to one day visit the old house.

He placed a flat palm against the lower corner of the wall space, just above the wainscoting, and tore off a sizable chunk of the wallpaper and carefully stuffed it into his pocket; it would be something else to show his friends and family, a back-up souvenir in case the bones weren't there.

A scream rang out, ear-shattering. As Chase jumped in his reaction, the reality of the movie's setting seized him, surging all through him.

It was Bruce, standing outside the window, peering through the chipped glass of the sash windows. His wily black hair and animated face were glowing in the afternoon heat.

"Where's my chainsaw, little girl?" he shrieked maniacally, cackling, looking every bit like the kind of B actor that would be cast for a low-budget horror movie.

"Uncle Bruce!" LaMonica yelled, clamping a hand across her chest. "You SCARED me!!"

"My name ain't Bruce! It's Leatherface!" He continued to howl, his black eyebrows and thick sideburns in blurry motion as his head bounced up and down. Chase took in the moment, appreciating for the first time Bruce's presence on this trip, though it wouldn't last long.

"Ohhhh!" She gathered herself and exhaled loudly, in exaggeration. "I should have totally expected something like this!"

"Whatcha got there, Killer?" he called out. "I saw you stashing something in your pocket."

Chase looked down at his pants, then randomly up at the ceiling, eager to focus on anything besides Bruce. "Just a piece of wallpaper. You know, a souvenir."

"Hmmm. Did you guys find the *real* souvenir yet? The little item that you really came here for?" Bruce folded his arms across the splintered windowsill, his eyes twinkling as he stared at Chase.

"No. We haven't gone out to the trees yet," said LaMonica. She took another big breath, then shoved her hair out of her eyes. Her voice shifted as she looked out the window, just past Bruce. "Where's Candy? You didn't just walk off and leave her, did you?"

"Here I am!" Candy suddenly appeared, nudging in beside Bruce, her equally frizzy hair and wide smile filling up several of the window's panes. They looked like the perfect couple. "Brucie has been showing me the sights!" She poked at his sideburn with a long blue fingernail. "I love it out here." Chase didn't want to know what she meant by that.

"Uncle Bruce, do you want to borrow this?" La-Monica asked, holding the camera out. "Get a few pictures for yourself?"

"Nah," he said, batting a playful hand at Candy's nails.

"You sure?"

"I'm sure. I wouldn't even know how to work today's cameras. Besides," he said, turning to completely face Candy. "I've got my own little movie star right here to chase around! Right, baby?"

He put her in a play headlock, rubbing a fist across her brown tundra-like hair, the whole giggly mess just sickening Chase all the more. *They've probably been out in the woods,* he thought with disdain. *Playing chase-me-with-your-chainsaw or some other perverted game.*

"Come on, loverboy," squealed Candy, pulling Bruce's arm. "Let's go and try to find the graveyard."

"There's a graveyard here?" LaMonica asked.

"Well, I think there's one mentioned in the movie so we're guessing there's one here somewhere," Bruce said, letting himself be slowly pulled away. "I saw a little clearing off to the side, back in that little area where we entered." He shot Chase a quick, devilish stare. "If we find any of those bones we'll let you know!"

Chase was stunned. "You aren't seriously going to look for them, are you?"

"And don't be trying any monkey business with my niece," Bruce called out, now being pulled by both arms. "Or else ol Leatherface will come getcha!"

He mimicked the sound of a live chainsaw, *wahhh-wahhh,* as they stumbled off. Chase wondered how many other forty-four year-olds behaved in such a juvenile way.

LaMonica picked right up on his disgust. "Look on the bright side. He's transporting all of our stuff."

"Yeah. Sure." *Which I'm still regretting.* LaMonica's dad was originally going to drive in from Phoenix with a mini U-Haul and load up a chunk of their college possessions, the things that they finally wanted to take back home. Clothes, dozens of books, two microwaves, a blender, all of it packed away in seven large banana boxes. Everything set, LaMonica had said, her dad was more than willing to foot the bill.

But a few days before his departure, his back went out, throwing the whole trip to the curb. LaMonica's cousin volunteered to drive down to San Antonio from Dallas in his pickup but then his work schedule changed, and that idea was gone. Chase and LaMonica decided to just rent a U-Haul and do it themselves. But then the day before the trip, Bruce and Candy showed up at LaMonica's graduate dorm in Bruce's deluxe-sized van, looking to help, looking for a laugh, looking for the next adventure. "I heard ya'll might be needing a van!" he'd exclaimed upon seeing them. "That true?"

"He just drives me nuts," Chase said flatly. "That's all."

"He's always driven you nuts. He's *Bruce*."

Yeah. *Your uncle.* My annoying neighbor. The one that always went too far with horseplay and roughhousing. Putting me in a headlock, laughing and rolling around in the grass. Teasing me with that stupid song, 'Chase and LaMonica sitting in the tree.' Running around the neighborhood with his stupid camera, taking random pictures of people, laughing when he got them by surprise. *The imbecile that I shouldn't even be around right now.*

"Have you noticed the way he drives?" he asked. "Weaving in and around other cars, like he's Evel Knievel?" Chase was getting heated and was fighting the desire to blurt everything out to LaMonica, to finally tell her everything. "And are we going to listen to anything besides ZZ Top?" The van's center console was chock full of rock CDs and cassettes, and for the last one-hundred miles ZZ Top had been the band of choice.

"Just ask him to put something else on. I even think he has some INXS, believe it or not." She chuckled as she leaned down to get a better look out the window. "They sure ran off quick. I think maybe Candy dragged him down to your little hiding place." She laughed again.

Chase knelt beside LaMonica, eagerly looking for a sign of them. "They better not be doing that. You didn't tell them it was the only oak tree in that area, did you?"

"No, of course not. On the ride here, he just heard the words 'tree near the house' and nothing more. I never said 'oak tree.'" She tugged at a dangling piece of mildewed wallpaper, and then looked back at him. "Do you really think there's something out there?"

"We're about to find out, I guess." He tapped his foot on the rickety hardwood, and looked out the window again, assessing the sky. Nighttime wasn't far off. "Ready to head upstairs?"

***

For Chase, there was plenty to be happy about. He and LaMonica were finally having the bulk of their college gear hauled back to Arizona, at no charge. His first year in graduate school at San Antonio State had just ended, classes out for the summer. A part-time internship at Bank One was waiting for him in Phoenix. Life didn't present many challenges.

And he was finally visiting the site of the chain-saw massacre, a lifelong dream, maybe even walking away with a souvenir, albeit a sick one. For most of Chase's undergraduate years, one of his resident hall counselors often told the story of a hidden bundle of animal bones on the film's location, something his grandfather—a low-level set laborer on the movie— tucked away for posterity but never returned to acquire. Everyone in the dorm hall talked and joked about it, but from what Chase could tell none had the odd interest that he had in the bones. The macabre movie prop would look good in his graduate dorm, hanging right alongside his *Psycho* and *The Omen* movie posters.

Upstairs, they walked from room to room, poking through the dusty closets. They speculated over what the upstairs was used for during shooting, since the majority of the film was shot downstairs. The same butcher paper was taped across the wallpaper, though much of it beginning to droop and fall; the rooms still had window shades, though they were ripped and stained with humidity and age. Chase assessed each window, trying to determine which one the film's star leaped from in the movie.

The rooms seemed dimmer, even dustier, and Chase came to a stop, his eyes falling across the shadows and emptiness. He fell back to 1980, walking through Bruce's cramped garage apartment, dark and dingy, ashtrays and beer cans lying about. A massive lava lamp stood watch. Bruce lay on the sofa, smoking something, while LaMonica dug through a plastic laundry basket, crammed with athletic gear. She finally pulled out a pair of baseball gloves, crying out "Here they are!" But Chase was fixated on a stack of

Polaroids. They were lying atop a Fleetwood Mac al-
bum, various pictures of the kids in the neighborhood,
some playing catch, others on their Big Wheels or in
someone's tree house. What caught his eye were three
pictures of Sherry, Chase's sister, in her dance leo-
tard, in their backyard practicing for her recital.

Little eight-year-old Sherry, holding her baton. A
close-up of her legs and waist. Another picture of her
chest and neck. Another close-up of her from behind.

"Come on, the ball's in your backyard," LaMonica had said, headed for the door. But Chase just stood
and stared at the pictures, his ten-year-old mind
shocked and numbed by the audacity of their presence.

"You better go, sport," Bruce lazily called out
from the sofa, then blowing a chute of smoke out into
the room. "Looks like Monica's got baseball on the
mind."

Chase had slowly exited, staring at this oversized
child lying on the sofa, confused and shaken. He now
stood at a bedroom window, running his knuckles
across the tattered window shade. LaMonica was
headed downstairs, walking out to the van to get her

water bottle. But Chase remained perfectly still, envisioning the pleasure of pushing Bruce right through the glass. No, better yet, guiding a live chainsaw cleanly through his kneecaps. And *then* pushing his helpless ass through the window.

Once downstairs, Chase stopped just past the front door jamb, noticing a three-inch jagged gash across the door trim on the outside. He stood in amazement, wondering how he didn't see the marking before. It was roughly neck-high, right across the splintered trim. He heard footsteps slowly crunching through the dead grass, followed by a voice confirming the weight of the steps.

"Wow. Is that an actual mark from the chainsaw?"

Without turning, Chase replied yes, that it was something he'd once read about in a magazine article on the film's director, Tobe Hooper.

"No kidding?" Bruce just stood out in the yard, hands on his hips, grinning, eager for more conversation.

"No kidding."

"Cool. Pretty interesting."

Total silence. Chase slid a pinkie through the groove, taking pleasure at the way he ignored Bruce;

he felt the pleasure at paying his former neighbor back, for the too-many headlocks and the horseplay, at the way Bruce held him down in the grass and made him say not just uncle but *uncle Bruce*.

"You, um, haven't said much since me and Candy picked you two up this morning. How you liking San Antonio?"

"It's good," Chase finally said, turning slightly to face Bruce, throwing him a bone.

"Cool. I figured you were. I know that LaMonica sure does. My brother tells me that she's always getting ready for a test or something." He ran his thumbs up and down over his bushy sideburns, scratching them out of habit. "Yeah, you two have done real good. Reckon once you graduate you'll put Phoenix in your rear view mirror for good."

Chase continued to trace his fingers through the groove, saying nothing.

"Wish I'd stuck with the whole college thing. I just didn't have it in me."

"You were once pretty good at taking pictures," Chase said. "Weren't you?"

"Huh? Oh. Yeah. You mean back when I used to run around in our neighborhood with that camera?

Yeah . . ." His voice faded as he looked off in the direction of the woods.

"You know," Chase said slowly, measuring his words. "Photography? Maybe you could get back into it. Take some classes or something."

"Nah," he grunted. "I'm pushing 45 as it is. I'll be a house painter until the day I die. Probably still be living in my brother's garage apartment."

LaMonica's voice rang out from the van. "Uncle Bruce! Where did you put that big bottle of Gatorade?"

He turned to look at the van, then yelled out something about a white shopping bag, back by the spare tire.

"What? Where?"

He shook his frizzy head and started walking for the van. "Girl couldn't find her own ass if both hands were tied behind her back."

Chase watched Bruce shuffle off, his boots kicking through the briars and thick scrub, off to rescue LaMonica from her thirst. Maybe he'd keep walking past the van, Chase hoped, continue on until he reached the chipped state highway. Maybe take a break and lie down across the yellow stripes for a while.

Out in the grass, Chase picked up a pecan twig and walked out to the edge of the woods, deciding to do a full sweep of the vast yard, see if he could spot the path to the graveyard. He jabbed the stick into a fat anthill, stirring up the insides. The sun had dropped low, and the horizon had slid into a warm blanket of yellow and purple, though the heat remained tenacious. *In the movie did Leatherface ever run around in the yard?* Was he always inside the house? Chase strained to remember as he walked, the grainy images of rural chaos sprinting through his memory. Leatherface running blindly through the kitchen, wielding an oversized hammer. Leatherface chasing a shrieking Denise down the hall, waving his chainsaw left and right. *God bless Leatherface,* something Bruce howled out his window when they first pulled into the turnoff in search of the house. Idiot.

At the far end of the yard he stopped and peered through the trees, at the thicket of brown leaves, a dead stump blackened by heat and rot. The years of being Bruce's neighbor flooded through Chase. All through childhood. Then—though it was less—middle school and high school. He swung the stick back and forth, its tip whisking through the grass like a swingblade. Then he stuck the stick down into the dry ground and pressed hard until it snapped in two.

He now approached a dead stretch of grass that ran up against the back corner of the house. Nearby was a trio of azalea bushes, knee-high, the skeletal branches long bereft of anything green. The words from his resident hall counselor chirped to life. *Walk about one-hundred feet away from the right-hand back corner of the house. Then, look off towards the trees to your right. You'll see the only oak tree in that area. That's where it is.*

But Chase could hear voices, and he knew he didn't need to count off the footsteps. The others were already there.

"Killer, is that you over there?" Bruce called out.

Chase turned towards the voices and walked towards the tree line, some thirty yards away. Bruce said something else, which made Candy giggle, and then he called out again. "Don't worry, my man. We didn't touch a thing!"

Chase could now see the blurry colors of their bodies through the thicket of tree limbs, LaMonica's yellow T-shirt, Bruce's blue jeans. He made his way carefully through dangling dead vines, masses of briars, a cluster of elm trees, and finally found the lone red oak, at the base of which stood Bruce, Candy, and LaMonica. They were all craning their necks, looking up at the branches.

He wiped a glob of sweat from his nose while LaMonica shot him a quick smile. "Hope you don't mind, Chase. I just told them it was the only oak tree in this area. We weren't going to climb it without you."

He shook his head and touched the skin of the tree, jubilant that the tree was actually *here*, right where his dorm counselor had said it would be. The ground smelled of dried acorns, many of them mashed down into the soil by the foot traffic of the others.

Candy looked at Chase and snickered. "So where is this thing? Tied to a branch?"

"The guy that told me about this just said that the bones were up really high. That's all I really know. Tied to a branch, yes." He wiped his nose off again,

224

this time dried his hand on his pants. "I think they're in a small bag." He suddenly became skeptical and wondered if one of his dorm hall companions had made a trip to the house after all, beating him to it.

LaMonica whipped out the camera and took several shots of the tree, then one of Bruce and Candy while they posed at the trunk, doing the whole giggly routine.

"Honey, what if nothing's up there?" Candy said, swinging at a cluster of mosquitoes. "I think I'm gonna head back to the van." Bruce just shrugged and continued to walk around the base of the tree, peering up through the leaves.

"Well," she said, walking away. "I'll see you guys back there. These insects are killing me." She smacked her arm in pursuit of a mosquito. "We're taking off pretty soon, right?"

"Yes, darling," Bruce muttered in slight irritation, his neck still stretched upward. "Killer, we're not going to be able to see it from down here. If it's up there, that is."

"It's up there," Chase said with conviction, hoping his conviction wouldn't prove to be embarrassment. "I'm going to climb up and find it."

He assessed the daunting height of the tree's lowest branches, which were as high as a basketball goal, and he didn't know what to say. But then there was Bruce. "Here," he said, stooping down, lowering and locking his hands together, offering Chase a boost up to the tree's first rungs.

After a strong upward thrust, Chase grabbed a branch, propelling his body upward; he planted a foot on a solid limb and amidst the plethora of tree branches found himself stepping up another two, already going higher and higher.

"Damn, boy, who taught you how to climb like that?"

Chase said nothing and stepped up another three rungs on the tree's ladder, now a good twenty feet off the ground. He came to a stop, leaning his chest against the tree, resting. A fat cluster of dried acorns dangled down, just near his right elbow. Above, the tree continued on for another seventy or eighty feet, and he squinted hard through the leaves and limbs, searching.

LaMonica called out that she too was headed back to the van, needing more film for the camera. Chase remained where he was but peered down to the trunk, unable to see much of anything but a jumble of criss-crossing branches and brown oak leaves. He looked back upward, then continued on, climbing even higher.

"Killer?" Bruce called out. "You okay up there?"

Chase grabbed a limb and pulled his body up, finding a new pair of branches for his feet. He looked left and right, down the length of every branch in the immediate area. *Freakin' wild goose chase. How stupid am I going to look?* He glanced down to the ground. "Yeah. I'm fine."

"See anything?" Bruce asked.

If I did, wouldn't I say so? Overgrown idiot. He rubbed a palm across the tree's rough bark. "What did LaMonica say she needed?" he called out. "More film?"

"Yeah. She ran out. She kinda went nuts, taking all those pictures of me and Candy."

Chase lightly banged his palm squarely against the bark, then went for it, weary of how predictable so much of life's conversations were. "So why did you give photography up?"

"Huh?"

"What made you quit taking pictures? You know. Photography."

A thin breeze skipped through the leaves, the acorns lightly swaying. Chase strained to hear Bruce's breathing while he gathered his words.

"I just . . . I just stopped. You know? I guess I was never really *into* it. You know what I mean?"

"But you were. When LaMonica and I were kids."

"Yeah. Kind of."

Despite the distance and the maze of tree branches that lay between them, Bruce's voice seemed clearer, almost louder. Chase went up another two branches, positioning his feet on the limb that his hands had just been on. Again he rested his chest against the core of the tree, breathing in a little quicker.

"I remember it clearly," he called out, as loud as he could. "You had all those pictures in your garage apartment. They were spread out on your record player and ironing board. On the kitchen table."

"Yeah," Bruce said with a snort. "Those pictures." He muttered something else that Chase couldn't pick up.

"You had a lot of pictures. Of a lot of people in the neighborhood." He checked down the length of a limb and before he could check the other side a blackish blur caught his eye, a banana-shaped bag, tied to a tree branch, just a few feet above. But for the moment he didn't budge. "Do you remember?"

Seconds passed before Bruce finally spoke. "Yeah. I remember."

The tied string snapped easily and Chase gently held the bag in his palm, the control of it seeming to spread to the control of the conversation. The fabric was purplish-white, bleached by years of heat.

"What do you remember?" he asked, while poking a finger at the bag's surface.

There was nothing for several seconds, not a solitary sound in this pocket of Williamson County, Texas.

"Did you, um, hear me?"

"You're asking me what I remember about the pictures?"

Another breeze flitted through the leaves and limbs and Chase took his time before answering. "Yes. That's what I'm asking you." At first he had been straining for strength but now the words just flowed.

"Yeah. You're right. I had a lot of pictures from people in our neighborhood. But I think I know which ones you're talking about."

Chase reclined his back against the tree, tapped the bag gently against his leg. He looked through the extended branches, on past the tops of the surrounding trees until his eyes found the upper portion of the house. It sat there, baking, the thin white clapboards splintered by the relentless sun.

He realized that Bruce had been talking for a few moments.

"There were all kinds of different pictures. Kids playing kickball. That old Chevy that I used to have. I've forgotten about most of them. But I definitely liked taking pictures. That's all."

He paused, then his voice shifted. "But yeah, Killer . . . there were probably some pictures that I shouldn't have taken."

"You had some pictures of my sister. Didn't you?"

"Yeah . . ." Bruce's voice cracked, then faded, sounding to Chase as if he had buried his face in his hands. But then he continued. "I know that you know it."

"I've *known* it," said Chase, looking out at the house again. A buzzard, large and ugly, sat on the house's top edge, taking in the emptiness of the land-scape.

"Uh-huh," Bruce mustered, his voice now loudly whimpering.

"I've never forgotten it."

"I'm so sorry, Chase."

"And I'm sure that I will never forget it."

"Oh, man," Bruce said, his voice now really quiv-ering. "I'm so sorry . . ."

Chase said nothing else. A final breeze kicked through the Texas twilight. The buzzard suddenly vaulted into flight, working his wings through the gray air. As he began to make his way down, Chase could hear Bruce continue to sob, and he wasn't sure how he felt about that.

***

The highway was nearly empty on the ride out. The van chugged across the warm asphalt, slowly passing a Colonial Bread truck, then an old Volkswagen. In the backseat Candy sat beside La-Monica, the bag of bones on top of a magazine spread across their laps. The bones ranged from tiny to large, the size of a tooth to the size of a finger. Bruce drove while Chase curled up on a sleeping bag, in between the boxes that were all crammed in the back.

"What in the world," Candy said, while examining a thin sliver of a bone, "would possess someone to stick bones in a bag and tie them to a tree?"

Holding a napkin, LaMonica picked through the pile, careful not to let anything touch her skin. "The more I look at this, the more morbid it gets. I wonder if there's any value to these things."

"Well, if there is," Candy said, "ya'll can buy us dinner, girl!" She snickered loudly, then nudged La-Monica with her elbow.

Chase squirmed left to right, and was finally able to get more comfortable. He looked at Bruce, who drove on in silence, slowly accelerating the van. As the women continued to speculate over the bones, Chase looked out the window, at the passing pastures and mile markers that shot by in the dimming light. He'd been thinking about volunteering to drive the next morning. Though Bruce had proudly announced that he was up for driving the whole distance, Phoenix was still over five-hundred miles away. The driving would be better off divided up.

Chase turned back to Bruce, who was looking at him in the rear view; their eyes parted ways, quickly back to where they had been, roaming. But then Chase looked again, once more meeting Bruce's eyes, and he forced a quick smile. Bruce held his gaze for a brief moment, and finally said, softly, "hey Killer ..." The words were audible, though barely, over the chatting of the two women. The two men then maneuvered their eyes and thoughts elsewhere.

The van rolled on at a steady seventy-five. The last of the sun's upper rim slipped behind the southwestern horizon. Chase closed his eyes and envisioned the great Leatherface running amok, swinging his giant chainsaw in every direction. In the dining room, with his family. On the staircase, chasing the hapless blonde. As Chase fell into a nap, he wondered how Bruce's van handled on the highway, how it would fare in the early morning hours of west Texas traffic.

ABOUT THE AUTHOR

John Glass is a playwright and a short story writer. He has had over twenty short stories and poems published in literary journals. John also runs *Student Plays*, a youth play business that carries scripts for 5th grade through college. This is his first collection. You may contact John at **john@johnglass.org** or read about his ongoing work at **www.johnglass.org**.

www.ingramcontent.com/pod-product-compliance
Lightning Source LLC
Chambersburg PA
CBHW071502170626
46811CB00007B/2693